Married to the Man that Stole My Innocence 2

Nikki Rae

Acknowledgments

First, I would like to give an honor to God for creating me with a writing talent because it wasn't for Him, none of this would be possible.

Secondly, I wanna thank my boyfriend Bernard and my three kids Ja'Neah, Sa'Niyah and Nasir for being patient with me as I take this writing journey. They listen to my ideas, my storylines, and sometimes they even help me pick my character's names.

I would also like to give a very special shout out to my Publisher Tyanna Coston, for recognizing my talent and making me a part of her team. Tyanna has helped mold me into the writer I am today. She has been everything that I could ask for in a publisher. She's not just a publisher, but she's also a friend and one of my biggest motivators.

Also, I can't forget about my pen sisters. They proofread for me, making sure they keep it a hundred with me at all times. I couldn't picture myself being with any other writing family outside Of Tyanna presents because my writing family rocks.

Now I wanna give a personal and special thanks to two special cousins, Tata and Josette, for being my biggest supporters. Since the day my writing journey started, they've been rocking with me from day one, making sure to be the first ones to get a copy of my books and read them from start to finish.

And lastly but most importantly, I want to thank my fans.

I want to thank each and every individual who has taken the time to open up any of my books and read them. Without you guys, I would have no reason to write. So thank you guys so much for rocking with me the way that you do. I love you all from the bottom of my heart.

xoxoxxoxo

Synopsis

Zaire Price just made Nyla his Mrs., solidifying his happily ever after in the process. Unfortunately, not even twenty-four hours after Nyla becomes Mrs. Zaire Price, a secret emerges that threatens to wash it all away like a high tide. This secret is bigger than any sandcastle either of them could have ever built.

In the dark about what her husband has done, Nyla basks in the ambiance of the honeymoon stage. Meanwhile, Zaire is carrying the burden of this secret around, scared of its repercussions. Will he take his skeletons to the grave to be buried along with him? Or will he attempt to be honest and lose everything he's worked so hard for?

Cameron and Tasha have the relationship everyone wishes for in public. However, now that they're expecting their first child together, things couldn't get better. Or so it seems.

Despite the love and adoration Cameron showers her with, Tasha can't help but to vie for the attention of someone from her past. But things aren't how they used to be. Will Tasha give up her knight in shining armor and her family to seek what she's been craving?

Chapter One

Zaire

Nyla and I have been married for exactly one month. Most people think we would be having the time of our life, but how could I enjoy my wife when I'm keeping a secret that I knew would tear us apart? If the secret ever got out, not only will the secret ruin my marriage, it would also ruin my life. I had too much to lose for that, but keeping this secret could do just as much damage holding it in. How could I tell my wife that I believe I was the one that raped her and stole her innocence? Although I was forced to do it, I still did it, but it was a matter of life and death.

It's also a night that I'll never forget.

"Yo, Zeek, we getting ready to get lit in this bitch. You see all these fine ass women up in here? We're gonna all get some ass tonight," my boy, Bishop, said, calling me by my nickname that everyone called me in high school.

Bishop was a few years older than I was, but it turned out that he was the dumbest of the crew. The night in the Poconos was lit as hell, and I was having so much fun that I wasn't worried about fucking no bitches. Hell, I was so drunk that I doubt that I was even capable of performing.

We left the party early, and when we got outside, we started walking behind some girl that was ahead of us. She was stumbling and didn't look too good. Bishop snatched the girl from behind. Everyone else we were with was laughing, but I didn't see shit funny. I was unclear about why the hell he was snatching the girl.

"Just lay her stuck-up ass right there and fuck her crazy, Zeek. We're gonna stand here and watch you put in that work. Then you'll officially be one of us," Bishop demanded.

"Man, I didn't sign up for no rape," I told Bishop.

"Nigga, who said anything about rape? I put something in her drink, so she won't remember a thing. Zeek, just do it cause if you don't, then we'll have to kill you because I can't afford for you to run your mouth. I felt something hard against my back. I silently turned around, and Bishop had a gun pointed at me.

"Man, get that gun off me. This shit ain't even necessary, just give me a condom," I stated.

At that point, I was scared as hell. I had never had any trouble with the law, and I didn't have no pussy in me at all. However, being drunk out of your mind, having a gun pointed at you, with a group of niggas waiting for you to do the wrong thing, had a way of making you fold.

I started to tug at her pants, and she began to move around a little bit to get away from me.

"If that bitch keeps moving, slap the shit out of her!" Bishop yelled.

"Please stop. Don't do this to me; I'm a virgin," the girl said lowly.

"I'm sorry. He has a gun pointed at me and says he'll kill me. I don't want to die, but I swear I'll be as gentle as I possibly can, I promise. I don't want to do this no more than you do," I whispered into her ear.

I kept my word and was gentle as possible, but I hated what I did to that girl. I felt like I was the one being raped. Bishop had like this brotherhood group, at least that's what I thought they were. It turns out they weren't nothing but a bunch of losers. I haven't seen or heard from them since that night. They tried reaching out, but I ignored them.

I knew I had to talk to someone about it because keeping it in was changing me for the worst. No one besides the people that was there and Dr. Bridgette knew what I did. Not even my brother knew, and I definitely couldn't tell him no shit like that.

******

I was on my way to pay Sharee a little visit. I needed to know why the fuck was her and Mike at my house, and what was her dealings with Mike. I had a few people keeping surveillance on her. She didn't think anyone knew where she was, but I did, and I was about to make my appearance. I had on a navy blue hooded sweat suit. I parked up the block and walked down. I wanted to go in by myself, but I wasn't alone. I walked around to the back and knocked on the door. I knew she was home because my people told me she was there and that she rarely ever leaves home.

"Who is it?" She asked, but I didn't answer. When she pulled the door open, she looked like she had seen a ghost. I pushed Sharee into the house and closed the door behind me.

"So, would you like to tell me why the fuck you and Mike were in my house Sharee?"

"Zaire, I can explain. Just please don't kill me," she pleaded with her hands in the air like I was holding a gun on her.

"Sharee, cut the shit. You know damn well I'm not here to kill your simple ass. Now back to my question. What the fuck were you and Mike doing in my house?"

"Mike wanted the songs that Teddy wrote. A month after you dropped Teddy, he started working with Mike," Sharee stated.

"Those are my fucking songs, so why the fuck were y'all gonna steal them? And when the fuck did you start working with Mike?" I snapped. Sharee took a hard swallow before speaking.

"Mike was my boyfriend; he sent me to work with you. I was supposed to start fucking with you and build your trust so I can help take you down. But once I started fucking with you, I fell for you, and I just couldn't do it. I even got my ass beat by Mike for never having any information. When you started fucking with that bitch and left me alone, I had no reason not to help Mike."

"Wow. So you've been a slimy hoe from the beginning and now look? You got your little boyfriend killed. If I was a street nigga, I would kill your simple ass right now. Who the fuck else is in on this? Because none of this shit doesn't make any sense."

"The only ones that knew about it were me, Mike and Teddy. I swear," she said. But something in my gut was telling me there was more to the story.

"Stay the fuck out of my life, Sharee. I should turn your ass in for this shit. I'm glad I didn't fall for your trick ass," I told her before storming out.

I got in my car and decided to take my yellow ass home. I was gonna try my best to be the best husband I could be. I needed to decide whether I was gonna tell my wife that I believe that I'm the man that raped her or would I live a lie and take the secret to my grave. When I pulled up to the house, Nyla's car wasn't there, and I wondered where she was at since she didn't tell me that she was going anywhere. I walked in the house and pulled out my cell to call Nyla, but she was already calling me.

"Hey, baby. Where you at?" I asked as soon as I picked up the phone.

"Hey, baby. You didn't get my text? I just left to meet Brandon at the hospital; Mariah is about to have the baby," she stated.

"Oh shit! What hospital are you going to, I'll meet you up there?"

"Virtua in Voorhees," Nyla replied.

"Aight I'm on my way," I said before disconnecting the call. Although I'd rather spend some quality time with my wife, I decided to go up to the hospital with her.

Chapter Two

Nyla

I just got to the hospital to support my brother and his firstborn. I couldn't believe I was about to be an auntie any moment now. When I got to the waiting room, Brandon was already in the back. I guess I was the first one to arrive at the hospital since no one else was in the waiting room. I text Brandon to let him know that I was there. While I was waiting, Zaire walked in, looking sexy as hell. I've been married for a month, and things were great, outside of the fact that I thought we would spend more time together. I thought we would have more sex since we were newlyweds, but for some reason, he seems to work more.

"Hey, baby. I missed you so much today I decided to take a much lighter workload. I need to spend more time with you," Zaire stated, hugging me. I swear it seemed like he could read my mind.

"I missed you too, baby. I'm glad you'll be home with me more."

"So, what's going on? Did she have the baby yet?" Zaire asked.

"I'm not sure. I text Brandon to let him know I was here, but he hasn't responded yet." I looked up, and Ariel and Mariah's parents were walking up. After speaking to everyone, we all took a seat and waited for Brandon.

"Wassup, sis? I miss you; we need to link up soon," Ariel said.

"I miss you too-" Before I could have a chance to say anything else, Brandon walked out, and I could tell by the look on my brother's face that something was wrong.

"Mariah had the baby, but they had to do emergency surgery on Mariah. I'm not sure what went wrong because I had to leave the room. They said a doctor will be out to talk to me as soon as they know something," Brandon explained with tears in his eyes.

I hugged my brother tightly and tried my best to console him. Mariah's parents were upset, asking Brandon questions that he didn't have the answer to.

After sitting for over an hour, we still didn't have any answers to what was going on with Mariah or the baby. I was stressed the hell out, so I could only imagine what Brandon was going through, not knowing what was going on with his first born and the woman he's in love with. A doctor finally came out.

"Family of Mariah Samuels?" The doctor said. Brandon and Mariah's parents spoke up.

"Ms. Samuels lost a lot of blood during the delivery, so we had to do emergency surgery. We are doing everything that we can, but right now, Ms. Samuels is in a medical coma. As far as the baby, he's doing great. If you want, you can see him now," the doctor said.

"Is my daughter gonna be okay?" Mariah's mom asked.

"Right now, it's touch and go, but we're doing everything that we can," the doctor answered. Brandon went back to meet his son while the rest of us stayed behind and waited. I felt sorry for Brandon and Mariah's parents. I knew this couldn't be easy.

I couldn't help but think about me and Zaire and when it came time for us to start our family. I prayed that Mariah pulls through. I would hate for Brandon to become a single dad. Me and Ariel went back to meet our nephew. When I got to the back, I washed my hands and picked him up. My nephew was the cutest thing. He was just perfect. He didn't look like Brandon or Mariah to me; he just had his own look.

"Hello, auntie's baby. I'm your auntie Nyla, and I'm gonna spoil you so much," I cooed. And this is your auntie Ariel," I said, holding him up to see Ariel.

"Hey, Chummy," Ariel said, giving the baby a nickname already.

After Zaire went to peek at the baby, Brandon insisted that we all head home and get some rest. He said he would call us if anything changes. After saying our goodbyes to one another, we headed home. The ride home was quiet. I didn't even bother to turn the radio on. I was just in deep thought as I drove behind Zaire. My phone ringing brought me from my thoughts. When I looked down, it was Tasha.

"Hey, bestie. Wassup?" Tasha asked as soon as I picked up the phone.

"Shit, I'm on my way from the hospital. Mariah had the baby, but apparently, she lost too much blood. They had to do surgery, and now she's in a medically induced coma," I told Tasha.

"Oh my God, what about the baby? How's Brandon holding up?"

"The baby is perfect. Brandon is doing the best that he can do, you know how my brother is. Of course, he's hurting and don't know what to do with himself. He told us to go home and he'll call if anything changes. It's just him and Mariah's parents up there."

"Damn, that's crazy. I hope she pulls through for real. That would really fuck Brandon up if she doesn't."

"Yeah, I know. We just have to pray for the best. Anyway, what's up with you?"

"Nothing much. I was just calling to see what you were up to. I wanted to do lunch tomorrow."

"Well, when I get in the house, I have to make sure that Zaire doesn't have anything planned. Then I'll let you know if tomorrow is good for me or not," I told Tasha.

"Aww, look at you sounding all married and shit, but aight, just let me know, " Tasha replied before we disconnected the call. I just pulled up to the house, and all I wanted to do was eat, shower, and make love to my sexy ass husband.

When we got in the house, we must have both been thinking the same thing because that's exactly what we did. Right after we ate the spaghetti that I cooked before going to the hospital, we took a shower. Zaire picked me up, carried me to our bedroom, and made love to every part of my body. Tonight would definitely go in my book of our best time. Once we were finished, Zaire rolled over to his side of the bed and pulled me to lay on his chest.

"I love you so much, Nyla Price. How did I get so lucky with you?"

"I love you too, Mr. Zaire Price, and we both know how you got so lucky. You stalked me," I told him playfully. "Nah, I guess we're both lucky because you complete me, Zaire." Zaire kissed the top of my forehead. The room fell silent for a moment.

"Zaire, do you have anything planned for us in the morning?"

"Actually, I have to be at the studio by nine tomorrow. I have a meeting then, but I should be finished by eleven, and on my way home, I'll probably stop by to see my mom. So, I should be home by one the latest. Then I need to have you all to myself," Zaire said, kissing my lips.

"Okay, cool. Tasha wanted to grab some breakfast tomorrow. So, I'll chill with her tomorrow and meet you back here around one as well." I grabbed my phone off the nightstand to let Tasha know it was a go. After I sent my text, I plugged my phone in, laid on Zaire's chest, and fell asleep.

*****

The next morning, I woke up when I felt Zaire get out of the bed. Usually, I'm up and out the house before him, but today he had to remove me before he could get up since I was laying on him. I grabbed my phone to see what time it was, and I saw that it was eight o'clock. I saw that I had a few text messages, but the group text from Brandon caught my eye over the others.

Big Bro: *Hey, y'all. I just wanted to keep y'all updated. Mariah is awake and seems to be doing fine. Thanks for being here for me. I love y'all more than you could imagine.*

Me: *Good morning, Brandon. I'm so glad to hear my sis is good. I'll be up there a little later and I love you too.*

Ariel: *Hey, bro. I'm so happy to hear that. I was worried to death. When I get off work, I'll be by there. Love you, and I love you too, Nyla.*

Me: *I love y'all too. I'll get up with y'all later. I'm about to get dressed to go to breakfast with Tasha.*

Big Bro: *I'll see y'all later I'm about to go get showered while Mariah's parents are still here.* After I clicked out of our group chat, I checked my other messages.

Bestie: *Hey, bestie. I'm just getting up, what time did you wanna link and who's driving?*

Me: *I'm just waking up too. I'll be there in about an hour or so, and I'll drive.*

Bestie: *Aight, cool. Let me get dressed.*

I picked Tasha up and we decided to go to Bob Evans. I was in the mood for their food this morning, and Prego didn't really care where we ate, her ass was just hungry. When we got to the restaurant, I pretty much knew what I was ordering.

"Hi, welcome to Bob Evans. My name is Natalie and I'll be your server today. May I start you off with something to drink?" The waiter asked.

"Yes, I'll have a coffee for now," I told her.

"And I'll take a large orange juice," Tasha ordered and the waiter walked off to get our drinks.

"So, bitch, how's married life?" Tasha asked.

"Honestly, I thought it would be a little different, but Zaire has been acting kind of weird since the night of the wedding. Right after we had sex, he started acting weird as hell, but when I ask him what's wrong, he says nothing. Then he's always working, but last night he told me that he cut back on work so we can spend more time together. I hope that he does because I was starting to get worried."

"Girl, y'all will be fine. Being married is hard work and new to both of y'all. At least it seems like he recognized there was a problem and now he's trying to fix it. So, I'll say that's a good thing."

"Yeah, I guess you're right. So, how's everything going with you, Cameron, and the pregnancy?" I asked.

"Girl, that nigga be stuck up my ass, and when he's at work, that nigga stay calling. The pregnancy is going great. I just turned four months. I'm supposed to find out what I'm having next month, but I think I want to have a gender reveal."

"Yes, girl. I'm gonna throw you a small gender reveal, and the biggest damn baby shower money can buy," I told Tasha excitedly. I was happy I was going to be a God mom. I wasn't sure when I was gonna be ready to have kids. I just got married, and I honestly wasn't ready to share my husband with kids right now.

"Yess, bitch. I know you know how to throw a good party. I'm excited about being a mother, but I'm also scared. I don't know the first thing about being a mom," Tasha expressed.

"You're going to be a great mother Tasha. Plus, I'll be there every step of the way so, my niece will be just fine," I stated.

"Your niece, huh? I am kinda hoping it's a girl, but I'm grateful for whatever as long as they're healthy," Tasha replied. I just nodded in agreement.

After we finished our breakfast, we decided to head up to the hospital to see the baby and check on Mariah. Well, I was gonna check on Mariah because, for some reason, neither of them cared for one another, but I had no clue why.

Chapter Three

Tasha

When we got to the hospital, I started getting nervous. That's been happening lately whenever I was around Brandon, but that hasn't happened since I was a teenager. I prayed for Mariah to recover because I would never wish ill will on anyone, but as far as I was concerned, she was the enemy. I loved Cameron, but Brandon was who I wanted to be with. In my mind, Brandon was the love of my life. The only reason why I wasn't with him was because of Nyla. I would never want to hurt her by dating her brother against her wishes. Her and I have had many conversations about Brandon dating her friends, and it was a no go for her. A part of me understood where she was coming from, but I was still in love with Brandon. Often you will hear her call Brandon my brother, but that's because she had no idea that I fucked him. I still remember the day it happened.

I just turned seventeen and Brandon threw me a small birthday dinner at the apartment we were staying at. Just after the dinner was over, Nyla, Ariel and myself had gone into our rooms for bed. I slept in the basement, but for some reason, I couldn't sleep, so I went back upstairs to get something to drink. Brandon was sitting on the couch watching a movie. I was only wearing a t-shirt because I wasn't expecting anyone to be awake.

"Hey, you good?" Brandon asked me.

"Yeah I'm great. I'm just thirsty as hell. What are you still doing up?

"I just wasn't ready to go to sleep yet. Did you enjoy yourself tonight?" Brandon asked.

"I really did. Thank you so much, I really appreciate you," I told him honestly.

"No problem, Tasha. You're family, and it's nothing that I wouldn't do for you and my sisters," Brandon stated.

"Look, Brandon, I need to tell you something. I appreciate everything you do for me because you didn't have to do it, but you do, and you're young yourself. I

know watching over and raising three teenagers isn't easy, but you make it look easy."

"Thanks, Tasha, and you're right; it's not easy, but it's gonna be okay in the long run."

"Brandon, I don't look at you as a friend. I've been in love with you for years, and I would love for you to be my first," I stated boldly. Brandon just looked at me like I was crazy at first.

"Tasha, I'm flattered, but I can't do that. I mean, don't get me wrong; you're pretty as hell but you're my sister's best friend. You and I both know that she won't be feeling that." Brandon tried to turn me down easily, but I wasn't having it. I wanted Brandon, and I couldn't think of a better time or a better person to lose my virginity to.

"Brandon, I love Nyla, but she's my best friend. I'm sure she would understand if we decided to be together but for now, what she don't know won't hurt." I climbed onto his lap.

"Fuck, Tasha. This shit ain't right. Girl, we can't do this-"

I wasn't sure where I got the balls from, but I kissed Brandon in mid conversation. At first, he tried to pull away, but I wouldn't let up. I took his hand and rubbed it across my ass. Brandon moaned in my ear and knew then that I wanted him. I got up off his lap, grabbed him and led him to my room. I felt like going to his room would be too risky. Brandon followed my lead. When we got downstairs, I made sure to lock the door.

I guess Brandon got tired of playing with my ass, so he took the lead. He pulled my shirt up over my head and tossed it on the floor. Brandon pushed me down on the bed and then stripped out of his clothes. I watched attentively as he stepped out of his boxers and let his pretty chocolate thickness hang free. My mouth damn near fell open at the size of his dick. Suddenly, I didn't feel as bold as I was moments ago.

"You sure you ready for this dick?" Brandon asked sexily while grabbing his thickness.

I shook my head yes, but the truth was I was scared as hell. It was too late for all of that, so I was ready for what was next. He covered my body with his chocolate muscular body and began to kiss me. The kiss was different from the one we shared upstairs minutes ago. It was more intense. It was the kind of kiss you saw two adults in love share on the romance movies.

Brandon took his time with me. He was patient and attentive with my body. He placed kisses all over my body, making me feel like I could never imagine feeling. He took me places that I didn't even know I could go. After exploring my body in every single way, he took my virginity. It was one of the greatest moments of my life. When he pulled out of me, Brandon kissed my lips and looked in my eyes.

"Are you okay?" Brandon asked.

With tears in my eyes, I shook my head yes.

"Tasha this was great, but we can't do this anymore," Brandon stated seriously. Deep down, I knew he was right, but being with him felt so right, so I couldn't understand what was so wrong about us being together. When Brandon left my room, I cried myself to sleep. When I woke up the next day, I couldn't even look at Brandon. Everything felt so awkward, but I was in love

and couldn't be with the man of my dreams without risking losing my best friend.

"Tasha, you good? You just zoned out on me," Nyla asked, breaking me from my thoughts of her brother.

"My bad, girl. Yeah, I'm good. I was just thinking about how in a few months, we'll be back up here for me to deliver my baby," I lied.

"I know, right. I can't believe you're about to have a baby."

"Girl, me either," I replied. Nyla went to use the bathroom, and I waited for her in the waiting room.

"Hey, Tasha. Wassup?" I heard Brandon's voice and I felt my stomach drop.

"Hey, Brandon. Wassup? Congratulations, I can't wait to see the baby," I told him.

"Thanks. He's beautiful, Tasha. I love him with everything in me already, and I haven't even known him for twenty-four hours yet. You'll see what I'm talking about when you have your little bundle of joy," Brandon stated.

"Yeah, I can't wait to meet my bundle of joy. I find out what I'm having next month, I just wish that you were the father," I blurted out of nowhere, feeling embarrassed as hell. *What the fuck was I thinking saying that dumb ass shit?* The room fell silent for a moment.

"Honestly, Tasha, I wish things were different myself. You're definitely a real one that I would have loved to have, but I could never hurt my sister," Brandon replied, shocking the shit out of me. As soon as I went to respond, Nyla walked out.

"Hey, bro. Wassup? You look a hell of a lot better than you did last night. I'm glad that you're feeling better," Nyla said to Brandon.

"Thanks, sis. That shit had me scared as hell last night. The thought of not knowing will have you fucked up. I was worried about the baby and Mariah, but I'm glad that everything worked out. Brandon told Nyla. All I could think about was me and Brandon. I wasn't sure why I was suddenly thinking about me and Brandon so much. What I did want to discuss was what he meant when he said I was a real one that he wanted on his team. Even though Brandon and I had sex multiple times for three months after my birthday, I didn't think he held the same feelings for me as I did for him. I had to find out what the hell this was.

"Tasha, do you want to see the baby?" Brandon asked, breaking me from my thoughts.

"Of course, I do," I replied, smiling hard as hell like Brandon just asked me on a date or something.

When the three of us got to the back where the babies were, I washed my hands, picked the baby up, and just stared at him for a moment. He was so handsome and precious. Slight envy came over me as I wished that I was his mother instead of that bitch, Mariah.

"What did y'all name him?" Nyla asked.

"We named him Kavon," he answered.

"I like that name," I said. I haven't even thought about names for my baby yet. I passed the baby to Nyla before going back to the waiting room. I knew I was being petty, but I couldn't handle being here with

Brandon and his son for much longer, without feeling some type of way. I sat in the waiting room waiting on Nyla. I wished I had drove my own car because I wanted to go home and take a nap. That was the one thing I hated about the pregnancy; I slept a lot.

Trying to get my singing career off the ground and still working as a makeup artist was becoming too much with this pregnancy. I became a makeup artist in the mall right after graduating high school and through college. I knew I wanted to have my own business at some point in life, so I decided to take a shot and open up my own beautician shop. I was making pretty good money in the hood. I had all types of clients. I planned to expand and do hair as well. I was also working on getting my hair license, so yeah, your girl be busy. I loved to sing. It wasn't a dream of mine, to be honest. I mean I knew I had a nice little voice, but I never dreamed of being a singer. Zaire was amazing and had so many connections. He worked with some of the biggest artists in the game. I knew Zaire had big plans for me, but after I do this tour, I plan to take a break or quit altogether. I wanted to focus on being a mother as well as my dream of owning my own shop.

Chapter Four

Zaire

It's been three months since I've been holding this secret in and it was eating me alive. I knew deep down that I wasn't going to be able to sleep until I told Nyla what I had done to her. I knew that I was gonna lose my wife, but I wouldn't be able to be much of a husband to her anyway if I kept this secret. I loved Nyla with all of my heart, but I needed to tell her immediately. I just pulled up to Dr. Bridgette's office. I knew she was the person I needed to talk to.

"Good afternoon, Mr. Price. How are you?" she asked.

"I'm fucked up," I stated, not holding any punches.

"Okay. Would you like to tell me what's going on?"

"I realized the night of my honeymoon that Nyla was the woman that I was forced to rape. That shit is eating me up inside and I'm sick to my stomach. I have to tell her because this secret is killing me," I damn near cried. When I looked up at Dr. Bridgette, she had her mouth open.

"Zaire, are you sure?" She asked, calling me by my first name.

"Yes, I'm sure," I snapped.

"I'm really sorry that this happened, and I agree you need to tell her. But you know this is going to cause major damage, probably beyond repair. Meaning you will probably lose your wife, and your secret will be out to the world. Because you know when people ask why she's divorcing you or separating from you so soon, she's going to tell them the truth. Zaire, this type of thing could ruin you forever. Are you sure you're ready for this type of heat?"

"I'm as ready as I'm going to get. I just hope that you can repair her and help her through this because she's really going to need you," I told her before storming out the office. She tried calling behind me, but I kept walking. I knew telling my wife this was gonna destroy her, but I hadn't thought about my career and family. I knew just who I needed to talk to. She was the only other person I planned to talk to before Nyla. And that was my mother.

I pulled up to my mom's place in tears. I felt like a baby in need of his mother. I didn't care how I looked or sounded. I banged on the door like the police and my mom snatched the door open. I just cried and hugged her tightly.

"Zaire, baby, what's wrong? You're scaring me," my momma asked, but I needed more time to cry and hug on my momma.

"Mom, I'm about to lose my wife. I love her so much, I don't want to lose her, but I fucked up badly," I cried.

"Zaire, what the fuck did you do?" I took a deep breath before speaking.

"About eight years ago, I was up in the Poconos with some people I considered friends. We went to a party, got drunk and one of the dudes I was with forced me to rape a girl at gun point. I didn't want to do it. I swear I didn't, but he said he would kill me if I didn't. I was so gentle with her and talked her through it, so neither of us wouldn't lose our life. Until Bishop wasn't feeling that I was being gentle, so he pushed me off and raped her as well. Nobody knows but you and the therapist that I was seeing when it first happened," I blurted. My momma was looking at me like I was crazy.

"Oh my God, Zaire. I can't believe what I'm hearing. You raped a woman? But where is this coming from?" She asked.

"Because I realized that night of my honeymoon that Nyla was the woman I raped," I confessed.

"Oh my God, Zaire. No, please tell me that you're not serious. That girl was worried about not being able to have sex with you because of her rape, and you're the rapist. Fuck! This is bad, Zaire."

"Mom, I know, but I have to tell her. It's been eating me alive."

"I'm so sorry, Zaire. I really don't have the words to say right now, but yes, you have to tell her. Just be prepared for the outcome because it won't be pretty," my mom told me.

"Yeah, I know, mom. I hate that nigga Bishop. If I was to see him, I would kill him for fucking up my life."

"Zaire, that wouldn't fix anything. You fucked up pretty bad, but now you have to deal with the consequences. You have to come clean, Zaire and tell Nyla everything. Yes, it will kill her at first, but you're gonna have to give her space unless she asks for something different. Everything will be on her terms and not yours, just be prepared," my mom told me. I sat and cried to my mom for a little longer before heading home to pack some shit.

I knew after I told Nyla what I had done that it was over, so I might as well get a head start. On the way home, I thought about how I would probably lose everything, including my freedom. God forbid if she wants to press charges. Nyla wasn't home when I got there, so I was able to pack the shit I needed the most before she got home. While I was putting my things in the car, Nyla pulled up. My stomach started turning and doing backflips.

"Hey, baby. Are you going somewhere? I saw you putting things in the car."

"Hey, baby. I think we should go in the house. There's something that I need to tell you, and after I tell you I know, you will no longer want to be with me."

"Zaire, what the hell is going on? You're scaring me," my wife asked, desperate for answers.

"Let's just go inside, Nyla," I told her.

When we got in the house, I had Nyla sit down. I knew it was gonna hurt her one way or another, so there was no reason to sugarcoat this shit.

"Zaire, tell me what's going on."

"Nyla, there's no easy way to say this, so I'm just gonna say it. About eight years ago, I was forced at gunpoint to do something that I didn't want to do, and it ruined two lives. I was made to rape a woman, and the night of the honeymoon, I realized that the woman was you." Nyla just looked at me in confusion.

"What did you just say?" Nyla asked calmly.

"Nyla, baby, I'm sorry I didn't want to do it. He made me do it or he was going to kill me. The night that we had sex for the first time is when I realized that it was you. The secret has been killing me, and I thought you should know."

The tears rolled down Nyla's face, and as bad as I wanted to kiss her tears away, I knew that I would never feel any part of her body again.

"Zaire, please tell me that this is some kinda sick, twisted joke that you're playing?"

I shook my head no as a tear fell from my eyes.

"Are you telling me that I'm married to my rapist?"

"Yes, and I'm sorry," was the last thing I said before Nyla busted me in the head with a lamp. I grabbed my head, which was bleeding.

"Nyla, I didn't want to do it! I'm sorry!" I pleaded, dripping blood.

"Get the fuck away from me right now, Zaire, before I kill you in here. LEAVE NOW!" She yelled and I walked out the door in pain. I knew staying would have only made things worse. I felt like shit. Like lower than low. The life that I once knew was over, and it was all because of Bishop's punk ass. I made a vowel to myself that I would not rest until I found Bishop and made him pay for what he did to Nyla, myself and probably others.

Chapter Five

Nyla

I was having a great day and couldn't wait to get home to my husband. Things have been going great with me and Zaire since we started spending time together. I really started to dig being a wife. When I pulled up to the house, I saw Zaire putting things in his car like he was leaving. I knew something was wrong with that picture. When I confronted him, and he said he needed to tell me something that he knew would end our marriage, my chest dropped to my stomach. I just knew that he was going to tell me that he cheated or maybe even had a baby on the way or something. I couldn't have been more wrong. Although I wished that I was right, it was much better than the truth. I went into shock when my husband told me that he was my rapist. I just couldn't believe my ears. I don't know what came over me, but I grabbed the lamp and hit him in the head with it. Once Zaire left, I stood there in shock, not knowing how to think or what to feel. I just cried and cried and cried all night long. I never made it to sleep or work; that's how fucked up I was. This was the first time I had ever done a no call/ no show at work, so my job was steady calling. I wasn't in the mood to talk to anyone, so I turned my phone off. After a couple of hours of replaying my attack over and over again, I finally drifted off to sleep.

I heard my doorbell, but there was no way in hell I was getting up to get the door. I had just made it to sleep. Now they were banging on the door, and I was getting annoyed, but I still wasn't getting up.

"Nyla, open this damn door! I know you're in there! I have to piss open the door!" Tasha yelled. I dragged myself out the bed knowing that she wouldn't leave. I opened the door without even speaking and walked back to my bedroom.

"Nyla, what the hell is going on with you? Why do you look like you've been crying all night? Wait, why aren't you at work?" Tasha asked question after question.

"I don't want to talk about it, Tasha. I just want to be left alone," I told her honestly.

"Oh, hell no. Nyla, what the fuck is going on? Did Zaire do something to you?" She inquired. Although I wasn't ready to talk about it just yet or ever for that matter, I took a deep breath.

"Tasha, sit down. This is some serious shit that I'm still processing my damn self, and I'm not ready for anyone to know, so keep your mouth shut," I warned.

"Bitch, what is it? You're scaring me."

"Zaire is the guy that raped me that night in the Poconos. He's the reason why my life was turned upside down!" I cried. Tasha was looking at me as if I had lost my mind.

"Nyla, what the fuck are you talking about? Why would you think that Zaire raped you? He isn't even that type of guy. You must have the wrong guy, Nyla," Tasha stated. The tears poured down my face. I wish that what she was saying was true, but it wasn't.

"Tasha, I hate to break this to you, but Zaire is the one that told me. He told me that he was forced to rape someone at gunpoint many years ago. The night of our wedding was when he realized that it was me that he raped. I'm sick to my fucking stomach. I married the man that raped me and stole my innocence. How crazy is that, Tasha?" I cried.

Tasha now had tears in her eyes. She just hugged me tightly and I cried my eyes out. I was sure that my eyes were already puffy from crying all night, so I knew I would probably look even more fucked up when I was finished crying this go around.

"Nyla, I don't know what else to say except I'm sorry that this happened to you. I wish I could make this go away and take away your pain. I will be your shoulder to cry on, just know that I'll be here no matter what you decide," Tasha consoled. I couldn't reply. All I could do was cry and rock back and forth.

After a few hours passed, Tasha made me shower while she got us food to eat. I didn't have an appetite, but she made me eat anyway. It was almost four in the evening and I finally decided to turn my phone on. I had a ton of messages from Zaire and a few from my siblings. I wasn't ready to talk to Ariel and Brandon about me and Zaire, but I knew if I talked to them, they would know something was wrong with me. They wouldn't leave it alone until I told them what was wrong. But I also knew that if I didn't answer my phone, they would pop up to my house.

Tasha stayed with me for a few more hours, talking and crying. As my best friend, she was there for me but knew when to give me space. After Tasha left, I just sat there. The more I sat there, the more I cried and thought about the night of my attack. I thought about how gentle Zaire was with me and how he really didn't want to do it. But it still doesn't change the fact that I was married to my rapist.

After sending a text to Ariel letting her know that I would call her when I got time, I powered my phone back off without waiting for a response. Before I knew it, I had cried myself back to sleep.

*****

It's been two days since Zaire dropped that bombshell on me, and I was in worse shape now than when I first found out. I couldn't eat or sleep nor have I been to work. I took a couple of weeks off because I really needed some time to process everything. The only thing I was doing was showering every other day. Other than that, I just sat around all day crying or sleeping. Zaire has been calling and texting, but I haven't looked at any of his text messages or listened to any of the voicemails that he left. The only person that knew what happened was Tasha, and I was even starting to push her away. I was knocked out on the couch when I was suddenly woken up out of my sleep.

"Nyla, get your ass up right now!" Brandon demanded, shaking me. I thought I was tripping at first until I opened my eyes, and Brandon and Ariel were standing in my bedroom.

"What are y'all doing here in my room? If I wanted company, I would have answered your calls," I stated before throwing the covers over my head.

"Nyla Marie Price, get your ass out this bed right now before I drag you out of this bed!" Brandon's voice echoed throughout the room. I knew at this point I had no choice but to wake up and tell them what happened with me and Zaire because they will never let me live this down. I got up feeling like shit, walked past the both of them, and went into the bathroom to take a piss and wash my face. When I got back to my room, neither of them were there. They were in the living room.

"Nyla, what's going on with you? You look like shit and this house needs to be clean. Where the fuck is Zaire?" Ariel asked. For some reason, Ariel's question caused me to laugh hysterically. Both Brandon and Ariel were looking at me like I was crazy as hell, and at this point, I wasn't sure if I wasn't crazy.

"Well, let's see. I don't know where Zaire is, neither do I care to know. Zaire packed up and left right after he told me that he was the one that stole my innocence.," I told them.

"Nyla, what the fuck are you talking about?" Brandon asked. The tears begin to form in my eyes. I knew I was going to have to tell them the story.

"Zaire was the man that raped me that night. He had no idea that it was me until our honeymoon. He held onto the secret for as long as he could, but it was eating him alive," I cried. I could see the rage forming in Brandon's eyes; it was a look that I've never seen ever in life. Brandon didn't even look like this when I told him about the attack in the first place. His look was scaring me to be honest. Brandon rubbed his hand across his face.

"Are you fucking telling me that Zaire, the man I just gave you away to, is the man... the man that raped you in the Poconos?" Brandon asked in confusion. I just nodded my head yes.

"Oh my God, Nyla. This is insane. I'm so sorry this happened to you; he doesn't seem like that kind of man at all. I can't even imagine how you feel right now."

Ariel started holding me tightly as I cried as if someone had died. I didn't understand why this was happening to me. I couldn't understand why God was punishing me. First, I lost my parents when I needed them the most. Then the very thing that I should have been able to give to whomever I wanted was ripped away from and taken by two men that I didn't even know. And lastly, I married the very man that raped me. Who the fuck does that?

"Which one was he?" Brandon asked. Both me and Ariel both looked up at Brandon, not understanding his question. "Nyla, which man was Zaire? Was he the man that was forced to rape you or the man that was the aggressor?"

"He was the man that was forced, Brandon, but what difference does that make?" I asked confusedly.

"It makes a big difference, Nyla. Look, I'm sorry that this happened to you, and this shit is crazy. I can't stay, I need to find that nigga," Brandon stated before darting out the front door. Brandon slammed the front door so hard that I thought my window was gonna break. Ariel tried to catch him, but it was too late, that nigga was gone. I wasn't sure what the hell Brandon was about to do, but I knew it wasn't good because I could see the darkness in his eyes.

For some reason, as angry as I was, I didn't want to see any harm to come Zaire's, way. I was still having mixed feelings about what I wanted to do when it came to Zaire. I mean, he was still my husband, and I was in love with him. I haven't thought about anything long term when it came to us or if there would ever be an us again for that matter.

"Nyla, please tell me how you are feeling?"

"I don't know what to feel; I just feel numb. It's like I can't feel anything. All I've been doing is crying and sleeping my life away. I haven't even been to work. I figured if I slept all day every day that I wouldn't have to face the truth. We have to find Brandon before he does something stupid that he'll regret."

"Honestly, Nyla, I don't think we should interfere. Brandon is gonna do whatever he's gonna do, whether we're there or not. If they do get into a fight, do you really want to see it? Brandon just had a baby. I doubt he'll do anything that will take him away from his son. We have to let them handle this as men," Ariel told me. In my heart of hearts, I knew she was right. There would be nothing I could say or do to stop Brandon from doing whatever it was he was gonna do.

Ariel went in the kitchen to make something to eat while I got in the shower. As I showered, I couldn't help but to think about my husband, and that night I was raped. I was starting to feel like I didn't have a right to be mad at him since he was pretty much a victim himself, but the other part of me didn't care because I was still raped, and that took a chunk out of my life. What I did know was, at this moment, the only thing I felt was numb. I knew I was alive, I could see and talk, but I couldn't feel anything.

Chapter Six

Zaire

"Zaire, what did I tell you when you first told me what happened? I told you to give Nyla some time to process everything, but no, your ass don't listen. Let me ask you something. What the hell makes you think what woman wants to see or talk to her rapist? I'll tell you, not a damn one. Now I'm not trying to be hard on you, Zaire, but you need to get your head out of your ass and let the girl be for now.

Believe me when I tell you, the two of you will talk again. It may not be what you wanna hear when y'all do finally talk, but you will have your chance to say what you need to say to her. You have to understand that it has to be on her terms and not yours. I love you, but tonight is the last night you can spend the night on this couch sulking. Go get you a room or stay with Cameron, but I can't enable you, Zaire," my mom said.

Ever since that shit went down with me and Nyla, I've been at my mom's apartment sleeping on the couch. Not because I didn't have anywhere to go but because it was comforting to me. But I understood that she needed her privacy as well, so I would just go stay at the place that I had near my studio. It had only been a few days, but I couldn't sleep or eat, all I wanted to do was be with my wife. Nyla wasn't answering my calls or texts, and when I called her job, they said that she hasn't been to work. I felt bad because I knew it was because of me. This was the second time that I came along and fucked up her life.

After talking to my mom a little longer, I grabbed my shit and bounced. Just before I went to my other spot, I stopped by the studio to check shit out. This was my first time here in days. I gave everyone time off with pay. I walked in and did my rounds then headed out the door. As soon as I locked the door and turned to leave, I was met with Brandon's fist to my face. I stumbled back, fell to the ground, and Brandon hopped on top of me, punching me repeatedly.

"I can't believe you're the one that raped my fucking sister!" Brandon yelled while beating the shit out of me.

"I didn't want to rape her, man! I swear I didn't. You can ask her, Bishop was gonna kill me if I didn't do it," I told him. He didn't say shit. He just hit me a few more times but finally standing up. He looked down at me with dark eyes.

"Stay the fuck away from my sister or next time I'll kill your ass," Brandon threatened before kicking me in my side and leaving me on the ground. It felt like my eyes were closing and I could barely see anything. I managed to get my phone from my pocket and call Cameron which was the last thing I wanted to do, since I knew I would have to explain why the hell Brandon beat my ass so badly.

"Yo Cameron, I need you to come pick me up from the studio, I'm in bad shape and I can't drive," I said into the phone.

"What the fuck you mean, you're in bad shape and can't drive? What the fuck happened to you?"

"Just hurry up, I'm in fucking pain. I'll explain later," I told him. What seemed like forever later, I finally heard a car pull up, and I knew it had to be Cameron.

"Yo bro, where the hell you at?" Cameron called out.

"I'm over here," I said loud enough for him to hear me. I swear everything seemed to hurt. I just wanted to take my ass home and get in the bed.

"Yo, what the fuck happened to you? Who did this shit?!" Cameron yelled, and Brian rushed over to help me up. Both of them helped me get into Cameron's car as I winced in pain.

"Cameron, call his wife and let her know we're on our way with him," Brian said.

"No, don't call her. We're not together right now," I stated lowly. "Just take me to my spot over this way."

Nothing else was said. Cameron drove me in his car and Brian drove my car. We pulled up to my place in no time, and I knew these two weren't going anywhere until I told them what happened. I would tell them just as soon as I took something for the pain and got settled. Once we got in the house, they got me some pain meds from my medicine cabinet. About a half hour later, the pain was finally dying down, and I put ice to bring down the swelling on my eye.

"Aight, enough of this shit, what the fuck happened to you? And what the fuck did you mean when you said you and Nyla weren't together? That's your fucking wife, how could y'all not be together?" Cameron demanded answers that I wasn't ready to give. I tried so hard to keep that part of my life away from everyone.

"Look, what I'm about to tell y'all ain't pretty at all, but I'm tired of keeping this shit in. About eight years ago, when I was chilling with Bishop and them, one night we went to a party in the Poconos. We were all drinking and having a good time. Then next thing I know, Bishop made me rape someone. He held a gun to my fucking head and threatened to kill me if I didn't rape her."

"Yo, what the fuck are you saying right now, bro?" Cameron interrupted.

"Just let me finish. The girl was a virgin and pleaded for me to stop, but I couldn't because I would have lost my life, so I talked her through it. I was as gentle with her as possible as I could have been. Bishop got mad that was being gentle and yanked me the fuck off of the girl then begin to forcefully rape her. I couldn't stomach to watch, so I ran off and haven't seen or talked to them since. I ended up needing therapy. That's how bad that shit ate at me. Long story short, I tried to put that shit behind me, but the night of the honeymoon, I realized that Nyla was the woman that I had raped," I revealed. They both looked at one another then at me.

"I know I didn't hear you say what I think you said? Let's go back a little. First, you said that you raped someone, then did you say that the woman that you raped was the woman you just married? I just need to be clear." Cameron questioned.

"That's exactly what I said, Cameron. To make matters worse, I told Nyla because I couldn't hold it in any longer, and that was days ago. I was at mommy's house because I didn't want to be alone and I wasn't ready to tell y'all about it."

"Yo, this shit is fucking insane. I don't even know what to say. You rape someone then married her?" Cameron quizzed in confusion.

"So, what the hell happened to you today?" Brian asked.

"Brandon showed up in a rage and just hooked off. I didn't stand a chance against him that's how angry he was. It happened so fucking quick that I couldn't land a single punch."

"Well, we can see that," Cameron sarcastically stated.

"Don't worry about his punk ass. He won't get away with this shit," Brian said.

"Nah, I'll deal with Brandon on my own, but what do you expect from the man. He just found out that his sister was married to her rapist. Hell, if I had a sister, I probably would have killed the nigga," I said honestly.

"I have so many different thoughts running through my mind right now that I don't even know what to say.

I can't believe that you raped someone and kept that shit to yourself then accidently married her. Like this is fucking crazy. I can't even imagine what Nyla is going through right now," Cameron said, really making me feel like shit.

Cameron and Brian was there a little while longer with me until I told them I just wanted to be alone. After my brothers left, I just laid there on the couch wondering how the hell did I allow my life to come crashing down. I lit me a blunt, thinking about how I was gonna find Bishop and what I was going to do once I found him. Bishop was going to pay for fucking up my life. I was mentally fucked up. I lost my wife, and now I'm physically fucked up. After I finished smoking, I took my ass to sleep.

It was two weeks later, and I still haven't spoken to or seen my wife or found Bishop. I hired a private investigator, but he had yet to find him. I was starting to lose myself and it was killing me. I called Dr. Bridget to make an appointment. As much as I hated to call her, I knew she was the only one that could help me deal with this. I was missing my Chocolate Drop more and more every day.

Today was the first week that I came back to work. I was supposed to have a few sessions with Tasha, but she hasn't shown up or answered any of my calls or texts. I heard what my mom said about giving Nyla space, but I needed to speak with her. I knew she wasn't okay, but I missed her, and I was really concerned about her state of being. I also thought it was time to pay a visit to Brandon. I wasn't sure what he would do when I showed up at his house, but it was a risk I was willing to take. The one thing that I learned about Brandon was no matter what the situation was, he was a reasonable man and always saw all sides to the story. I just know that if we talked, that could be the start of getting me at least a conversation with Nyla. So yes, she was worth another ass whopping.

Chapter Seven

Brandon

"Brandon, you have to relax. You've been worked up for the past two weeks. I understand that you're hurting for your sister but that don't mean you can just abandon your responsibilities as a father and a lover," Mariah bitched once again like she had been doing for two weeks.

I mean, I understood where she was coming from to a degree, but my sister was going through a really rough time right now. I loved my son and Mariah more than anything in this world, but at this very particular moment, my sister needed me more than they did. I still did my job as a father and as Mariah's man every day of the week. Now granted, I may spend a few more hours a day more than I would normally do, making sure my baby sister was good. Nyla was damn near like a daughter to me, and I didn't appreciate Mariah arguing with me every day for spending time with my sister. The crazy part was she could come with me. I was starting to get turned off by her selfish ways.

"Look, Mariah, I don't want to hear this shit every day when I come in. What's your problem with me making sure my sis is good at this difficult time? Tell me one thing that I'm neglecting at home? I still take care of you and Kavon, but you act like you can't come with me. She is your friend. Well, at least that's what I thought, but I don't know what to think of you anymore," I stated.

"What the fuck is that supposed to mean, Brandon?" Mariah asked angrily. Before I could answer her, the doorbell rang, and I was glad because I was over this shit. But I did wonder who the hell was at my door. I walked off, leaving Mariah standing there in the room. I opened the door and couldn't believe who was on the other side.

"Zaire, why the fuck are you at my door? You have a lot of fucking nerve showing up at my house after what you did," I snapped.

"Look, Brandon, I know that I'm the last person you want to see or speak to right now And if you want to beat my ass again, then go ahead, but I still need to speak to you," this nigga stated. As pissed as I was at Zaire, something in me wanted to hear him out. Hell, it had to be important if that nigga was willing to risk coming to my house after what he did.

"You have five minutes, Zaire. So I suggest that you make it worth your while and beating your ass again doesn't sound so bad," I told him.

"I'm just gonna get straight to the point. I know what I did to Nyla, but I swear I didn't want to do it. That nigga was gonna kill me if I didn't. He had a gun to the back of my fucking head. I hated what I did to that girl. It fucked me up badly. I did years of therapy trying to get past this shit. But I need you to know that I love Nyla with every fiber in my body and I miss her like crazy. I know this is crazy, fucked up, and unfortunate, but I want my wife. I can't live without her. Nyla completes me in a way that I can't explain."

I didn't even know what to say to this nigga. A part of me was ready to smash his face in, but crazily, the other part of me felt sorry for the man.

"I don't even know what to say to this. What am I supposed to say to the man that raped my baby sister? I prayed for years that I would find out who ruined my sister, so I could kill the bastards. But never in a million fucking years did I think that when I found him, he would be married to my sister. Zaire, you do realize how insane this is, right?" I snapped.

"Brandon, you don't think I know this shit is insane? You're just the one that helps her pick up the pieces, but how do you think I feel knowing that I'm the one that shattered her heart then put it back together, to be the same person to shatter it all over again? I feel like shit, but oddly enough, I feel like we can get through it.

It may not be the greatest love story, but I'm in love, and she's in love with me too. I want to have kids with Nyla. I don't care how long it takes; I won't stop until I get my wife back. I hired a private detective to locate the guy Bishop that forced me to rape Nyla and ruined both of our lives," Zaire poured his heart out. I was pissed at myself for actually feeling sorry for him. I guess I knew deep down that he was a good man and I really liked him for my sister.

"Look, I'm not sure what I can do. What I will say is I'll try to talk to Nyla, but she's really fucked up right now, so I don't think she would even consider talking to you. And nigga, let me know if you find that nigga because I want parts. He will not get away for what he did to my sister even if I have to kill him myself," I told Zaire.

"Thanks, Brandon. As soon as I get some info on that nigga, I'll hit you up," Zaire promised before heading out. As soon as I closed the door, when I turned around, Mariah was standing there with the baby.

"So, are you going to tell me what you meant before we were interrupted?"

"Mariah, please leave it alone. I have more important things on my plate, Mariah. I don't know why you keep making such a big deal out of me helping my sister get through a very difficult time? This shit is starting to turn me off," I stated as I walked up and reached for my son. I walked in the baby's room to spend some time with my little man as I did every night. After playing and cuddling him, it was time for his bath. After giving Kavon a bath, I lotioned him down, then placed him in my arms and sat in the rocking chair, reading him a story. I hoped Mariah wasn't still on her bullshit tonight because I needed to have sex to relieve some stress. When I walked in the room, Mariah was on the phone but quickly cut her conversation short when she saw me walk in.

"Who was that?" I quizzed.

"Oh, that was just Lexi," she replied. Something told me Mariah wasn't being honest with me. I've never known her to lie to me before, so I just let it go. I went and got in the shower, and when I walked back into the bedroom, Mariah was in her phone, smiling at whatever she was reading.

"I left the shower water on," I told her, and she jumped like I startled her. She plugged her phone up and went to get in the shower. Once I made sure she was in the shower, I grabbed her phone off the nightstand, and to my surprise, she had a lock on her phone. I knew then something was going on, but I didn't say shit that night. I was damn sure going to get to the bottom of what was going on within the next couple of days. I got in the bed and clicked off my light. I wasn't even in the mood to fuck anymore. I just took my ass to sleep.

The next morning, I decided to take off from work, but I decided to keep that my little secret. I was gonna see how my girlfriend moved when I wasn't around. I was never the type of guy that did this type of shit, but something in my gut just wasn't right. I did my normal morning routine, including kissing Mariah and the baby goodbye before heading out the door.

My life hasn't been the easiest, as I'm sure you've already read. Raising my sisters while I was damn near still a kid myself wasn't the easiest, but I made it work, and I think I did pretty good. Both of my sisters, as well as myself, were pretty successful. At the moment, I currently owned my own catering business, but I planned to open my very own restaurant. I loved my sisters with everything in me. The three of us were always close even before my parents died. To be honest, me and Nyla were probably closer than me and Ariel was, but only because Nyla was the baby. She just seemed to need me more than Ariel did. Ariel was more a free-spirited person who kept her life kinda private, meaning she would tell us what she had going on but only the things that wouldn't worry us.

Losing my parents killed me, but I had to be strong for my sisters. Hell, I even took in Tasha. Tasha was a different story though. I was in love with Tasha, but that was something that I knew I could never act on again. I just don't think that Nyla would understand. I didn't want to add any more shit to her plate, so I keep my feelings for Tasha tucked away.

I called my best friend, Joey, up and told him I needed to borrow one of his cars off the lot that he owned. Him and I have been best friends for the last four years. He was the only person I really fucked with outside of my sisters. When I pulled up to the lot, Joey was inside his office.

"Yo, what up? What the hell you need a ride for if your car is working?"

"I need it to spy on Mariah. I hope I'm wrong, but I think she's fucking around on me," I told him honestly. I'm gonna get to the bottom of it because if she is it's a done fucking deal. I don't play the cheating shit on no day.

"Hell, for her sake, I hope not either. But take whatever car you want and keep it for as long as you need to. Call me if you need me." I chatted with Joey a little longer before staking out from my house.

It was noon, and Mariah was walking to the car with the baby. After strapping him in, she got in the car. I found it strange that she hadn't called me to let me know she was going anywhere. Just before she pulled off, I called her.

"Hey, baby. I was just about to call you to let you know me and the baby was stepping out for a few hours. Lexi wanted to hang out with me and her God son," she said. I suddenly felt a sense of relief because she could have just said that she was home. Maybe I was overacting.

"Aight, kiss my baby for me. Y'all be safe, I'll call you a little later," I told her before we ended the call.

Mariah pulled off and I felt kinda of silly for doubting and spying on the woman I love. Damn near a half hour later, we pulled up to some park. I wondered why the hell would she drive so far to meet up with Lexi, especially since Lexi only lived ten minutes away. Mariah got out of the car and put Kavon in his stroller then walked over to a bench where a light skin guy was standing. The guy leaned in and kissed Mariah on the lips like that was her man. When she kissed him back, my blood started to boil. That nigga then bent down and picked up my son, and that's when I lost it. I couldn't control my anger.

I felt like a mad man, but I took a few deep breaths just so I could snap a few pics of what was going on. I let them get nice and comfy before calling Mariah's phone, but she pulled it out, looked at it and then placed the phone back in her bag. Just as I was about to hang up and walk over there, I could hear her talking. I placed my phone on mute to listen.

"Was that him?" the guy asked.

"Yes, that was him," she answered.

"This is fucking crazy. When the hell are you gonna tell him, Mariah? You keep saying you need more time, but how much time do you need to tell him that we're back together and Kavon's my son? I'm not with all this sneaking around shit anymore."

"Drew, I don't feel like arguing with you about us. Besides, I don't know for sure that Kavon is yours."

"He looks just like me, Mariah, but that's neither here nor there. I'm gonna help you take care of him one way or another."

"Can we talk about this another time? I just have a half hour to see you, so I didn't come to argue," Mariah stated. My heart was crushed. I was gonna get out the car and fuck shit up, but I had seen and heard enough. I hung up the phone and sped off.

When I got to the house, I immediately started packing all of their belongings. I was angrier and more hurt than I've ever felt in my life. I wasn't sure what I was feeling at the moment, but I felt like my heart was gonna stop. I packed the shit so quick and sat everything near the door. I didn't have much to say to her; I just wanted her gone. I called to make an appointment for a DNA because I may have been raising and got attached to a baby that wasn't even mine. I prayed that Kavon was mine because he was my world. I didn't want to think about what I might do if he's not mine.

About two hours later, Mariah pulled up to the house. My heart started beating fast and I begin to pace the floor. When she opened the door, she noticed the shit at the door immediately

"Brandon, what's all this shit at the door?" Mariah asked.

"It's your shit, Mariah. I suggest you call someone to come get your shit out of my house right fucking now. I really did love you, but I see you're nothing but a lying ass, cheating bitch." Her eyes got so wide that you would have thought they were gonna pop out of her eye socket.

"Brandon, what the hell is going on?" She asked dumbfounded, which only pissed me off even more.

"Get the fuck out of my house, Mariah before I do something I'll regret. You know exactly what the fuck I'm talking about. But since you wanna play dumb, let me show you." I shoved my phone in her face so she could see the pictures.

"When I get back, you better be gone," I told her before walking out the door. She just started crying, but I could care less about that bitch's tears. I couldn't believe she played me.

With no destination in mind, I just drove until I felt like stopping. When I finally stopped, all I could do was cry. I have never cried so hard in my life. I couldn't believe I was going through this shit right now. I needed a vacation, and soon because if not, I was gonna end up in jail. I decided to drive back towards home in silence and let my thoughts run wild. I needed to talk to someone, but I didn't feel right taking my problems to Nyla when she going through her own shit. If I was to tell Ariel, I'm gonna have to bail her out of jail tonight, so against my better judgment, I decided to call the one person that I knew I could talk to, and I knew could keep a secret.

"Hey, Brandon. What's up? Is Nyla okay?" Tasha asked when she picked up the phone.

"Hey, Tasha. I'm sorry to bother you, but I just needed someone to talk to, and I couldn't think of a better person than you. And yes, Nyla is fine, and I would appreciate it if you kept this between us. Can you meet up with me?" I asked.

"Yeah, I was just about to leave the shop. Where do you want to meet?"

"I'm starving, so how about Friday's?"

"Aight, cool. I'll meet you there in about twenty minutes," she stated before disconnecting the call.

After pulling up to Friday's, I sat in the parking lot and waited for Tasha to get there. My phone ringing brought me from my thoughts, but I instantly became infuriated when I saw that it was Mariah calling. I declined the call and tossed my phone on the seat, wondering where these bitches get their balls from.

Chapter Eight

Nyla

Today was the first day that I felt somewhat normal. I decided to go back to work, and it kept me busy, so I didn't have as much time to think about Zaire. Don't get me wrong; I thought about Zaire everyday all day. I hated it, but going back to work helped me think about him less. I wasn't sure what I wanted to do when it came to Zaire, I literally haven't seen or heard from Zaire since the day he left. I refused to talk to him or about him at this point. It took me an entire month to get where I am today. I haven't cried in a week which was great since I've cried every day, all day for the past three weeks. So, I would say that today was a good start for new beginnings.

I was on my way over to see Brandon. He asked me to come by after work for dinner, and since I'm not the one to turn down good food, I happily accepted. I knew it would feel weird being there and not seeing Mariah and Kavon. I couldn't believe what that bitch did to my brother, and I thought she was my friend. All I know is she better pray that me or Ariel don't catch that bitch because she was gonna get her ass beat. When I walked in the house, it smelled so heavenly. I always loved Brandon's cooking. He could really be like a five-star chef.

"Hey, sis. Come have a seat out here on the deck. I cooked your favorite," he stated as I took my seat at the table. Brandon made some steak, red roasted potatoes, and green beans and cornbread. I couldn't wait to dig in. After we said grace, I begin to devour my food. I didn't realize how hungry I actually was.

"Damn sis, you seemed a bit hungry," Brandon joked.

"Well, I can't help that my brother can cook," I told him. "So how are you Brandon? Have you talked to Mariah about the baby?"

"I honestly don't have shit to say to her. I haven't seen her since the DNA test. That should be coming in the mail any day now. Nyla, thank you for being there for me," Brandon said sincerely.

"Brandon, you don't have to thank me. Not after everything you've done to help me get through my shit. And just so you know, I'm beating that bitch's ass when I see her," I replied honestly.

"Deal, but if I could make one small request. Just make sure I'm there," Brandon said with a chuckle.

"You got it, bro. Anything for you," I told him.

"Look, Nyla, I know what I'm about to say is probably going to piss you off and dim the mood, but I feel like I need to tell you this. I've been in contact with Zaire, and I really think that the two of you should talk. Since the two of you have been separated, you're miserable, and I just want you to be happy, and Zaire makes you beyond happy. He's really sorry and miserable without you," Brandon stated, shocking the shit out of me. I don't think I quite understood what the hell my brother meant. I felt so betrayed. *Why would he sneak around my back with my rapist?*

"Brandon, what the fuck are you even saying right now? Please tell me that you didn't just say you've been talking to Zaire. Why would you talk to him, Brandon?"

"Look, I'm not good with sugarcoating shit. That's not my area, so I'm gonna say some shit that you might not like or agree with, but it needs to be said. After you told me what happened, I beat the shit outta that nigga and had planned to do so every time I saw him. The night before that shit went down with me and Mariah, Zaire came to see me and pleaded to talk to me, so I did. And all I'm saying is y'all need to talk. But let me say this, you might not remember much, but what you do remember is he was just as much a victim as you were. And I know that you think people would look at you crazy for working shit out and staying with him.

But fuck them, Nyla. Real love don't come around every day. Besides, you took vows with that man, and you can't even have a conversation with him? That's what grownups do, Nyla. They talk and y'all either gonna work it out or not work it out, but y'all need to talk. Both of you need to be heard."

"Brandon, how could you betray me like this? I thought you were on my side. I'm your sister," I cried.

"Nyla, I am on your fucking side, but that doesn't mean that you're doing the right thing. I don't like what he did no more than you do, but he was forced. If I was in that predicament, I'm almost sure I would have done the same thing. When your life is in someone else's hands, you do what you need to do. Avoiding the situation will not make it go away. Which is why I also invited him over so y'all can talk," Brandon stated, causing my heart to drop down to my stomach. Before anything else could be said, the doorbell rang.

I had so many mixed feelings about seeing Zaire. I was nervous, scared, and angry. I couldn't understand why the fuck would Zaire pull some shit like this. Hearing Zaire's voice from the house made me sick to my stomach that I literally threw up. Everything was just too much. Everything that I just ate and drank came up.

"Nyla, you good?" Brandon asked. I couldn't answer because I was puking. I felt someone grab my hair out of my face, and when I looked up, it was Zaire. I didn't know if I should push him away or thank him. As angry as I was that they ambushed me into talking to Zaire, I had to admit my husband was sexy as shit. Zaire was wearing a red V-neck t-shirt and a pair of jean shorts. He was wearing his favorite gold chain and watch. I swallowed hard before speaking.

"Thank you, but I got it from here," I stated, moving his hands from my hair. Silence filled the air, and nothing was said while he walked around to sit across from me. I looked up, and Brandon was no longer standing at the door.

"Hey, chocolate drop," Zaire spoke.

"Zaire," I replied dryly.

"Look, Nyla, I'm not gonna hold you long, but I need to get a few things off my chest. I know finding out that you married the man that raped you and destroyed your life isn't good news to digest. Please don't take what I'm about to say insensitive, but Nyla, this shit didn't just happen to you. It happened to me too. I never forgave myself for what I did to you that night. When Bishop had that gun pointed at me, I was scared as hell and would have done just about anything to stay alive. Until it was over and caused me to need therapy at that point, dying that night didn't sound too bad. I tried everything in my power to make it easy for you. But I need you to know that Bishop had made up in his mind you were gonna get assaulted one way or another. In a very strange way, you should be glad he didn't choose someone else to do it or things may have been a lot worse. Nyla, I love you with everything in me, and I miss my wife," Zaire said.

I couldn't believe the balls on this man. I hate to admit it, but I'm sure he's right. Whoever that Bishop was had made up his mind that he was gonna violate me no matter what.

"Zaire, you may be right about everything that you said, but that doesn't change the fact that you assaulted me and then married me. You wanna stay married and pretend this never happened? Is that what you're asking me, Zaire?" I cried. I didn't realize I was crying until I felt a teardrop fall on my arm. I wiped my tears and tried to get myself together, but I ended up crying so hard that I was throwing up again.

Zaire jumped up from the table and ran over to me to hold my hair once again, and for some reason, this time, I didn't reject him like I did the first time. When I was finished throwing up, Zaire held me tightly on his chest, and that only caused me to sob even harder. The smell of Zaire cologne and the way he held onto me made me realize how much I missed my husband's touch. This moment had me confused about what to do about my marriage. To be honest, up until tonight, I was sure that I was going to divorce him. Maybe even have him arrested, and now a part of me want to take him home and make love to him all night. Crazy, right?

I pulled away from Zaire's hold, looked up at him, and his eyes were full of tears. I was starting to feel sorry for him. Hearing Brandon talk about how this affected Zaire then hearing what Zaire said made me realize that I wasn't the only victim here. I still wasn't sure what I wanted to do, but it definitely had me in think mode.

"Zaire, I'm not sure how to feel or what to say to you right now. I can't deny the fact that I still love you and miss you like crazy, but what I do know is I'm not ready to decide. I need more time to figure this shit out. So, as of tonight, I can't say yes to your request, but I also can't find in my heart to say no either," I told him honestly.

"Chocolate Drop, I'll take that any day over a hard no. I'm not gonna stay any longer because I know this is already overwhelming for you. But just know that I love you and I'll do anything to get my wife back," Zaire stated while kissing my forehead. "Oh yeah, don't be mad at Brandon. He loves you and would do every and anything for you, even if you won't do it for yourself. I love you, Nyla. I hope to hear from you soon," Zaire replied. When he got up to leave, everything in me wanted me to ask him to stay, but I knew I couldn't. I just sat at the table as the tears fell freely from my face.

"Sis, I never meant to hurt you, but I really think that conversation was needed. Now whether you decide to work it out with Zaire is totally up to you. I just don't want you to make a lifetime decision based off of a temporary emotion," Brandon said. I knew he was right because Brandon has never steered me wrong so far.

"Brandon, I know you only want the best for me. I'm sorry for overacting. Thanks, you were right, I needed that. But I do need to ask you something," I stated, and Brandon raised his eyebrows.

"Do you really think I should forgive Zaire and stay with him?" I asked Brandon, desperate for his opinion.

"Honestly, sis, I do think you should forgive him and work on your marriage. Zaire is a great man and he reminds me a lot of myself. But most importantly, he loves, cherishes, respect, and appreciates you. Nyla, I know this is hard for you, but it's not the end of the world. Think of it this way, Zaire was your first, and if you honor your vows, he'll be your last, and that's a beautiful story. That Bishop nigga don't count and will be dealt with soon," Brandon answered.

"I guess I never thought of it like that, I love you so much, Brandon and I don't know what I would do if I didn't have you as a brother. I'll text you when I get in. I have to go; I gotta work in the morning."

"I love you too, lil sis. Be safe, and Nyla, remember the decision is yours to make. Just make sure you make the best decision for you," Brandon said, hugging me tightly.

When I got in the car, I heard my phone ringing and wondered who was calling. I looked down, and it was Zaire. I ignored the call because I needed some time to clear my head. Minutes later, I heard my phone ding that I had a text message.

Husband: Hey Chocolate Drop, I hoped that you answered, but I'll just text it. I wanted to tell you something else that I think you need to know because I don't want to keep anymore secrets. And if you decided to forgive me and take me back, I want to have a clean slate. So, I wanna put

everything on the table. That night you took me to meet Dr. Bridgette, you weren't tripping when you said things seemed weird. Dr. Bridgette was my therapist that helped me get through what I did to you. I also saw her once after the wedding because I needed to talk to her once I realized that you were the woman. I'm truly sorry for any and all pain that I caused you. I love you, Nyla.

I had to reread that text message at least three times to make sure it said what I thought it said. I couldn't believe this shit. It was just too much. As soon as I felt like I was ready to move forward with my life, I was forced to talk to Zaire. Then I found out we had the same therapist. I just sat in my car and cried for about ten minutes before I finally pulled off to go home. I didn't even bother to text Zaire back. When I got in the house, I texted Brandon to let him know that I made it in safely. I powered off my phone, jumped in the shower and then took my ass to sleep.

*****

Two weeks had now passed and I still haven't decided if I wanted to take my husband back or not. The only thing I knew was I felt incomplete without him, but I also felt stupid for still longing for him. Tasha was on her way over so we could hit the mall up and have some much-needed girl time. I swear it seemed like we didn't get to see one another that much. Honestly, I hardly spoke to Ariel like that. It seems like ever since she's been with Jasmine, she's been distant. I've been so busy dealing with my own shit to address it. The doorbell rang, and I knew it was Tasha. I opened the door for my bestie and my eyes fell on her baby bump. I couldn't believe Tasha of all people was having a baby by my brother in-law at that.

"Damn bitch, you finally showing," I said to Tasha. I can't

believe I'm about to be an auntie and a God mom.

"Girl, yes. I still can't believe I'm having a baby, but I better start believing since I only have a few months to go."

"I can't wait to throw this gender reveal next week. I told you I would make sure that you have a great reveal. Anyway, let's get out of here. I'm ready to do some shopping and stuff my face with some good food."

We pulled up to the mall in twenty minutes. I wasn't sure what store I wanted to go in first, but I knew I was coming to do some retail therapy, so I knew we would be here for a while. After shopping for what seemed like forever, me and Tasha had more bags than we could carry.

"Y'all too beautiful to be carrying your own bags. Y'all should let us carry your bags," a voice said.

Me and Tasha both turned around to see who was offering to carry our bags. My eyes locked with this tall caramel complexion guy that had a gorgeous smile and a nice build. He was dressed nice, and the guy he was with was also nice looking. Without waiting for an answer, both guys took our bags and walked us to my car.

"Thanks, sexy," Tasha flirted.

"The pleasure is ours. What's y'all name?" The tall Caramel guy asked.

"I'm Tasha and this my sister Nyla. What's your name?" Tasha answered.

"My name is Andre, and this is my brother Andrew, but my friends call me Dre," the tall caramel guy answered. Now that I took a closer look at the two of them and they do look like brothers.

"Well, it was nice to meet y'all, and thanks for helping us with our bags," I replied ready to get out the parking lot, so I could go eat.

"Can I get your number, chocolate?" Andre asked. For some reason, him calling me chocolate got to me, and it reminded me of Zaire.

"My name is Nyla, and I'm a married woman, so if you'll excuse me, I have somewhere to be," I stated before getting in the car. Tasha got in the car about a minute later, so I could only imagine what she was out there saying.

"Girl, what the hell was that about?" Tasha quizzed when she closed the car door.

"What are you talking about?"

"Why did you have to tell him that you were married? You won't be married much longer, so why tell him that?" Tasha questioned. Her statement pissed me off for some reason.

"I told him that because I am a married woman and who said I wouldn't be married for much longer?"

"Nyla, are you thinking about getting back with Zaire?" Tasha asked me, looking dead in my face.

"Honestly, I am. I was gonna tell you some of the shit that has transpired over the past two weeks. We can talk about it over lunch."

Tasha didn't say anything, she just put her seat belt on, and I pulled off. We pulled up to Outback Steakhouse, and I could smell the aroma from the food from outside. I was glad there was no line, so we were seated right away. We ordered our drinks and food at the same time.

"So, what changed your mind about Zaire?" Tasha asked, getting straight to the point.

"Truth be told, it was Brandon," I told her, and she looked at me like I had three heads. "

Brandon called me over a couple of weeks ago to talk, and when I got there, he ambushed me into talking to Zaire. I was mad at first and me and Brandon got into it, but I thought about what he said, and he was right. Shortly after, Zaire showed up. Things got intense and emotionally very quickly. And out of all the different feelings that I was having, the one feeling I was clear about was how much I loved and missed my husband.

Tasha, I know this may sound crazy, but Zaire completes me. I know what he did to me ruined my life, but he was also a victim. It's not like he chose me; he was forced at gunpoint. He was so gentle that night that if it wasn't for the fact that I didn't know him, you would have thought we were two people in love making love for the first time," I replied.

"Damn Nyla, that's deep as hell. I can only imagine what you're going through. All I can say is do what's best for you no matter what anyone else says. That's your husband and your life, so I say do you, boo. I got you no matter what you decide," Tasha assured.

"Thanks, bestie. You sound just like Brandon, I told her. Anyway, what's going on with you and my brother?" I asked. Tasha had a weird look on her face.

"What you mean? Did Brandon say something to you?" Tasha said, making me raise my eyebrows. *Why the hell would she have thought Brandon told me something? I thought.*

"Tasha, what the hell are you talking about? I was talking about Cameron. Why did you think I was talking about Brandon?" I quizzed.

"Girl, that's what I meant. I don't know why I said Brandon's name. But to answer your question, we're okay. He's great actually, I've just been feeling a little distant lately. I think it's the hormones, and everything just happened so fast with us, you feel me," Tasha stated. I knew there was something she wasn't telling me, but I decided not to make a big deal about it and change the subject.

"Anyway, have you been to the studio lately?" I asked curiously.

"Nah, that shit didn't seem right. I know I could be making money, but that shit ain't more important than our relationship," Tasha answered seriously.

"I feel you, Tasha, but make your money. You have a little one on the way, I don't expect you to let what I'm going through with my husband stop you from making money. I'm not that selfish."

"I'll think about going back to the studio, but in the meantime, I think it's time that you call your husband and see if y'all can get through this. Everyone can see that's your soulmate and you're his. I can't even front; I kinda envy y'all relationship. You have a love story that you only see on tv or read in a book. Usually, two people in love never have their happy ending. Nyla, there is no doubt in my mind that you can have your happy ending with Zaire. I mean, he was your first, why not make him your last? Go get your man, bitch," Tasha said, causing me to blush.

"I think I may do that," I told Tasha. We paid for the bill and headed home.

Chapter Nine

Six months later

Zaire

"Who gives this woman away?" The pastor asked.

"We do," Cameron and I said in unison as we gave our mother away to Charles. My mom had finally got all her shit together. She had an office job and all. Charles moved her out of that raggedy ass apartment and into a house. Me and Cameron brought her a car, and she couldn't have been any happier. The wedding was small and intimate since neither of them had large families. After giving her away, Cameron and I stood in our places. The church doors opened, and when we looked up, it was Brad's ass walking in. Brad started clapping his hands loudly.

"Well, hello, Candy. Surprised to see me?" Brad said with a chuckle. "So, you think that you can ruin my life and my marriage then live happily ever after? Well, I'm here to put that shit to bed," he said quickly, pulling out a gun. Everyone started screaming.

"Yo, you need to get your ass out of here," Charles threatened.

"Look, man, I don't have no beef with you, so stay out of this," Brad replied and raised his gun. Brad pulled the trigger, and Cameron jumped in front of my mom as bullets rang out, hitting Cameron. And I heard my mom let out a scream I'll never forget. I thought she was screaming because Cameron was hit until she hit the floor with blood seeping through her once white dress. More gunshots rang out, and Brad's body hit the floor hard and loud. When I looked up, Charles was holding a gun. I held my mother tight while praying that she pulled through. She had so much blood, but I couldn't see from where.

The ambulance and cops finally arrived. This shit looked crazy with three bodies sprawled at a wedding inside of a church. All I could do was cry. My brother and my mom was hit by the nigga that was supposed to be my father. I could care less if that nigga lived or died. When we got to the hospital, I was a total wreck. The worst part was playing the waiting game.

"Baby, I'm sorry that this happened. Everything is gonna be just fine, I know it will, "Nyla said while rubbing my back. Nyla and I have been officially back together for four months now. At first, we took it slow and dated to get used to being around one another again. At first, the shit was awkward, but now things were better than ever.

"Thanks, baby. Where's Tasha?"

"She's on her way. She had to find a sitter for the baby."

"He has to pull through. He just had a baby, this shit ain't fair," I cried. I walked over to my aunt Pat and Brian, who was also crying. Today was crazy as hell. I knew my aunt was going through it, her sister, nephew, and husband's life was on the line. Although my aunt Pat and Brad were still separated didn't mean she didn't care if that nigga died. They were married for years.

I was waiting for Charles to finish up with talking to the police, and I was sure I was next to give a statement. This shit was frustrating and overwhelming.

I needed a blunt like right now, but I didn't want to leave the room until I knew what was up with my moms and brother. An officer came over and got my statement. Once I was done, I saw the doctor walking out. I couldn't read his face, but I hoped like hell that my family was good. Nyla walked over and put her hand on my shoulder to comfort me.

"Family for Price?" the doctor called out.

"Right here," I answered.

"What's your relationship to the patients?" The doctor asked, pissing me off.

"Look nigga, this my mom and my brother. What difference does that make? We're all her family, can you just tell us what's up?" I snapped.

"Both your mom and brother will make a full recovery, but we need to keep both of them overnight for observation. They are both very lucky to be alive. The bullet that hit your mom was very close to a main artery that could have killed her immediately. The bullet that hit your brother went through him and into your mom. You can go back to them now; they're both in the same room. And because of the nature of the incident, y'all all can go back at once, just try to keep it down," the doctor stated.

When I got to the back, I couldn't help but drop a few tears. I was so happy that I didn't have to bury my mom or my brother. I would have lost it if something would have happened to either of them. We all were talking and surprisingly able to muster up a few laughs under the circumstances. Someone walked in, and when we turned around, it was a doctor.

"Is there a Patricia Maxwell in here?" The doctor asked.

"Yeah, right here," my aunt answered.

"I'm sorry, but your husband didn't make it," the doctor stated. The room fell silent, and my aunt closed her eyes as the tears ran down her face. Brian ran over to console his mom as we all just stood there and watched the two of them grieve. I wasn't sure how to feel, to be honest. Even though he was the reason we were all here in this hospital, he was still my dad, and he did raise us just as our uncle. I felt bad for Brain and

Aunt Pat. This entire day was overwhelming, and I needed to go home, get out of these bloody clothes and smoke a few blunts. Twenty minutes later, we said my goodbyes and headed out the door.

*****

Later that evening, when I woke up from my nap, I noticed that Nyla wasn't lying next to me. I used the bathroom then went to find my wife. I found her in the kitchen whipping up some dinner. I wasn't sure what she was cooking, but it was smelling good as hell.

"Hey, baby. How are you feeling?" Nyla asked.

"I feel like shit to be honest. I feel like this is one big nightmare," I answered honestly.

"I can't even imagine how you feeling, but I hope you're hungry," Nyla said while setting a plate of food in front of me.

"Yeah, I'm starving."

Nyla made some fried chicken wings, mashed potatoes, and corn with some fresh lemonade. I wasted no time digging into my food. That shit was hitting, and it was just what I needed. After we finished eating,

I went out on the balcony to smoke a blunt. While I was sitting out there, I called the hospital to check on my mom and Cameron. They were both doing well, which I was happy to hear. Charles was a great fit for my mom, and I grew to like him a lot. Although every time I see him, I think about the image of him beasting out my mom. For some stupid ass reason, that shit was embedded in my memory. When I walked back into the house, Nyla was sitting on the couch flipping through the channels. She stopped at the news station that was talking about the shit that happened earlier today.

"Baby, can you change the station? I'm not ready to deal with the media's shit right now." Nyla did what I asked her with no questions asked. For the rest of the evening, Nyla and I watched movies and chilled until we both fell asleep on the couch.

Chapter Ten

Tasha

"Shit, Tasha! You about to make me cum," Cameron groaned while hitting it from the back. I threw my ass back on his dick, meeting his every stroke. "Fuck, I'm cumming!" Cameron yelled, releasing his seeds inside of me.

"Oh God, Cameron! I'm cumming too!" I cooed as I released my juices on Cameron's inches. After we both came, Cameron just stayed inside of me and kissed my back.

"Tasha, I love your ass, you know that?"

"I love you too, baby," I told him honestly. I truly did love Cameron; the problem was I was in love with Brandon. Brandon and I have become extremely close ever since the night he called to meet up. I've crossed the line a few times with Brandon and I feel horrible for it. We haven't had sex, just some kissing, and intense touching. It was getting harder by the day and Brandon was all I could think about.

The baby's cries through the baby monitor ended our moment. Cameron pulled out of me and put on some boxers to attend to our daughter. Serenity was now three months, and she was beautiful. I loved being a mom more than I imagined I would. Cameron was beyond a great father; I loved the way he interacted with Serenity. It had been a little over a month since Cameron and his mom were shot at the wedding. That day was one of the worst days of my life. I thought I was going to lose Cameron, and the thought of losing him made me realize how much I truly loved him. If it wasn't for the act that Brandon was occupying a spot in my heart, Cameron and I would be perfect. I knew I had to stop doing the shit I was doing with Brandon because I was sure if Cameron found out, he would kill both of us. To be honest, for Cameron to be a straight-up guy that didn't live the street life, he was a pretty crazy motherfucker. Cameron would end a life or beat your ass without a second thought.

"There's go, mommy. She may be a little worn out because daddy just finished giving her a much-needed workout."

"Cameron, why would you tell her that? Give me my daughter fool," I told Cameron.

"What you don't want her to know that I be busting your ass in this room?" I thought I was free spoken, but clearly, Cameron had me beat. Cameron was right about one thing, that nigga fucking skills were like nothing I ever experienced. His dick was long and thick, and he knew what to do with it. Not to mention his tongue game could turn you out after the first few licks.

"What time are we going to your mom's?" I asked, changing the subject.

"We leaving around five, so make sure your slow ass is ready. I'll dress my Princess because I know if you do it, we'll be late," Cameron stated. That man knew me so well. His mom and that creepy ass man had gone to city hall and got married, and they were having a small dinner tonight. If it wasn't for Miss Candance, I wouldn't even go. It was something about that man that rubbed me the wrong way, and he made me feel funny every time I see him.

*****

We just got to Ms. Candace's house, and when we walked in, she was in the kitchen, so I walked into the kitchen to see if she could use a hand.

"Hey, baby. How are you? And where's my grandbaby at?" Ms. Candace quizzed.

"I'm good, and your grandbaby is with your crazy son," I told her. "By the way, congratulations."

"Thanks, baby. I just wished I was able to have the wedding I wanted, but thanks to that bastard of a baby dad of mine who ruined it just like he did my life," she stated, and I felt sorry for her because that was crazy.

"Hey, mom. This food smells good as hell. What time can we eat?" Cameron said when he walked into the kitchen, holding Serenity.

"Well, hello to you son, and your greedy ass can eat as soon as everyone gets here. Give me my granddaughter," she told Cameron while taking Serenity from Cameron's arms.

I loved his mom. I know she did drugs just like my mom, but at least she got off and got her shit together so she could build a better relationship with her sons. I didn't know if my mom was dead or alive.

Everyone was finally there, and it was time to eat. As soon as Nyla and Zaire walked in, Nyla picked Serenity up and hogged for damn near the rest of the visit. Right after dinner, Charles got up to make a toast.

"I just wanted to say thanks to each and every one of you that came to the wedding and the dinner. Although we didn't expect for the wedding to end up in such a tragedy, but thanks to the man above, we got through it, and now we're here. So, me and Candace decided to just go to the hall of justice. So, introducing for the first time as husband and wife, Mr. and Mr. Charles Maxwell," Charles announced while raising his glass. After everyone took a drink, Cameron stood up.

"Momma, I'm glad that you found someone to make you happy, and for his sake, he better make sure he keeps you happy. Because I would hate for you to become a widow," Cameron stated with a chuckle, but if you knew him, you would know that he was serious. I could tell that Charles didn't like his comment, but he didn't say anything he just wore a sly smile.

"I say all that to say congrats, momma. I love you," Cameron ended, and everyone clapped their hands. I smiled at him because Cameron was a piece of work and I loved every bit of it. Cameron didn't take no shit from anybody. He was sweet yet rude as fuck, and him being fine and sexy as hell didn't hurt much.

When I first met Cameron, I thought he would be just a fling and something to do when I was bored. But his rude ass managed to earn a place in my heart and give me my first child. As I sat and thought about me and Cameron, I knew that I had to stop doing the shit I was doing with Brandon. I was in love with Brandon, but he was off-limits. I had a good relationship with Cameron and I love Cameron to death. Hell, I may even be in love with him. I just think I'm so focused on the forbidden fruit that I haven't allowed myself to see what was right in front of me. And that wasn't fair to Cameron or my daughter. I owed it to Serenity to give her a two-parent home. I was being selfish. I had a good man and an even better father to my daughter, and I was willing to risk it over a childhood crush. I really needed to get my shit together.

Chapter Eleven

Cameron

"Hey, Cameron. I know that you didn't care much for Brad anymore, but will you be attending his service tomorrow?" My aunt asked as I was about to leave my mom's crib. I was waiting for the joke to be over because I knew she was playing with me.

"Aunt Pat, I know you not serious right now? With all due respect, that nigga almost killed me and my momma a few weeks ago, and now you want me to go to his service because that nigga supposed to have been my pops? Nah, I'm good on that. Honestly, if Charles hadn't bodied his ass, I would have done it after that shit he pulled."

"Damn bro, do you always gotta be so damn rude? All you had to do was say no. You always gotta be over the top. My dad did some fucked up shit that I don't like, but he was still my dad and y'all's too, to be honest. I get why you pissed off that nobody told you he was your dad, but damn, Cameron, have a fucking heart," Brian snapped. I guess he was tired of me talking shit about his dad. But what he didn't know was I didn't give a fuck what he was tired of. Brad was a fucking coward and I lost all respect for his ass.

"Look, bro, I'm sorry if you don't like my delivery when I talk about your pops, but I'm not like y'all. I don't easily just forgive and forget. This ain't no damn tv show, this is my life and my feelings. Man, fuck that nigga Brad and anybody that don't like what I have to say about that nigga," I stated. Before I could finish getting the words out of my mouth, Brian punched the shit out of me.

"Nigga, is you crazy?" I asked before slugging his ass back. By then, we were in a full fight. Everyone was trying to break us up, but that shit wasn't happening. That nigga was crazy as hell if he thought he was gonna punch me over his punk ass daddy. I couldn't lie Brian had hands for days. Zaire came over and was the only one that could get us apart. Zaire was a strong ass nigga. He was another one that could throw hands; I guess it ran in our blood.

"Y'all niggas need to cut that shit out, fighting in momma and them house like that. Both of y'all are some disrespectful ass motherfuckers. Everybody get the hell out!" Zaire yelled. The room fell silent because Zaire rarely ever snapped, so I knew we must have been tripping. Although I was still pissed, Zaire was right, so I decided to take the high road.

"My bad, I didn't mean to be disrespectful. I'm sorry I'm gonna go now and to answer your question, Aunt Pat. Nah, I won't be there tomorrow," I said.

"You know what your problem is, Cameron? You are just like Brad. His blood runs deep inside your veins. That's why you act the way you do," my aunt Pat stated, pissing me off even more. She had me ready to slap the shit out her ass. I just bounced without saying another word with Tasha on my heel. I hopped in the car and peeled off.

"Yo you need to calm the hell down, Cameron. Our daughter is in the car, so you need to slow down or pull over and let me drive. As a matter of fact, pull over, Cameron," Tasha demanded. I didn't feel like arguing, so I just pulled over and let her drive. I'm so sick of this damn drama all the time. A nigga need a vacation and soon.

As soon as we got in the house, I took my daughter out of her car seat to give her a bath and put her to bed. After giving my princess a bath, I just sat in her room in the rocking chair, rocking her to sleep. Serenity had a way of keeping a nigga calm. She was such a good baby, she rarely even cried. She had the brightest smile I ever saw, and that shit warmed a nigga's heart. Once Serenity was asleep, I laid her in her bassinet and went to take a shower. I walked in the room about to strip out of my clothes, but apparently, Tasha was already in there. I figured I'd join her and get some pussy while I was in there. Tasha's phone lit up, and I saw a text come across the screen from Brandon asking if she thought she could get away tomorrow afternoon. It looked like it was more, but I didn't want to open it because then she'll know that I read it. I was curious about what that was about. I got in the shower but decided not to hit it.

"I think someone called or texted your phone when I was on my way in here. Your phone lit up," I told Tasha.

"I wonder who that was," she stated. Once she was done rinsing off, she got out. Something didn't sit right with Brandon texting her. I know she said they were like brother and sister, but I've never heard her mention anything about them texting or talking. I stepped out the shower but left the water running. I walked to the door and she was on the phone.

"Brandon, you know you can't be texting me at this time of the night. He was in the room when you texted. But anyway, what's up? He's in the shower so I can't really talk. Aight, I'll meet you at the park around noon because I need to talk to you about something anyway, but I gotta go," she said, disconnecting the call.

I got back in the shower, pissed. *What the fuck were they up too?* I wondered. Whatever it was, I'm sure it was something that they weren't supposed to be doing. I rinsed off pissed the fuck off. I walked back in the room and she was laying across the bed. I dried off, put my boxers on and got in bed.

"That was Nyla texting making sure we were good," Tasha lied right to my face and as bad as I wanted to burst her bubble and confront her, I decided not to because I had a better plan.

"Oh cool," I said, getting into bed and turning out the lamp.

The morning came quicker than I wanted it to. I was actually tired and wanted to stay in bed. I looked over, and Tasha wasn't in bed. I used the bathroom, and when I got back in the room, she walked in with my princess.

"Good morning, daddy's baby. Did you sleep good," I cooed, taking my daughter from Tasha. This was a morning routine that I did everyday with Serenity before I went to work or started my day. I fed her, changed her, and played with her every morning. Serenity was my pride and joy and meant the world to me. I hated to have to leave my baby, but I was having a very important meeting this morning. I was now dressed about to head out the door. I kissed my baby and Tasha as I normally do.

"So, what do you ladies have planned for the day?" I asked.

"Not much, I'm supposed to link up with Nyla around twelve, but nothing after that. Probably come back home and make dinner. I'll see you later, baby," that lying heffa said.

I just went with it because I needed to be sure before I cut her hoe ass off. When I got to work, I didn't have that much time before my meeting was starting. I cursed myself for setting it so early.

My meeting ran over later than I expected, but it's all good. I just got a client that's gonna make my company millions, so it was worth every hour. I called Zaire because I really needed to talk to him. I called and he picked right up.

"Yo, bro. wassup?" Zaire answered.

"Yo, where you at? I need to come holla at you about some shit," I told him.

"I'm at the crib, come through," he answered.

"Aight, I be there in about a half hour. You by yourself or is Nyla home?"

"Yeah, she home. We took off to spend some quality time together, but you good," he answered, and that was all I needed to hear. I hung up and headed to Zaire's house. When I got to the house, Nyla was in the kitchen cooking, and that shit was smelling good.

"Hey, bro. Where's my sis and my Goddaughter at?"

"Wassup, sis. She was home the last time I talked to her. I just left work. I'm surprised you haven't talked to her today," I replied.

"Nah, haven't spoken to her since we were over to moms," she answered. "But I guess I'll call her a little later if I get some free time," Nyla said.

"Aight, cool. Where my brother? I just need to holla at him right quick, then I be out y'all hair," I told her.

"You good, my vagina could use a little break," she stated with a chuckle, shocking the shit out of me. I wasn't used to her talking like that. I just laughed and went to find Zaire.

"I'm surprised you ain't go to your pops service," I said to Zaire when I found him on his patio.

"Yeah, aight, nigga. You knew I wasn't going to that shit, but anyway, what brings you by?"

"Look, keep this between us. Don't say shit to nobody, especially to Nyla," I told him.

"I got you. Now, wassup?" He inquired.

"I think Tasha fucking around on me with Brandon," I told Zaire.

"Nah, she wouldn't do no shit like that, but what got you thinking that?" I told him everything that happened last night, including what Nyla just said about not talking to her since we were at moms. Zaire looked shocked and kept shaking his head. "It must be some misunderstanding. Call her and see where she is, I bet her ass is home."

I pulled out my phone and dialed her number. I put the phone on speaker and waited for her to pick up.

"Hey, baby. What's my princess doing?" I asked.

"Sitting here looking at me and Nyla talk," she said, and my heart dropped to my stomach. I had to keep it

together. I looked up, and Zaire had his mouth
hanging open.

"Oh, okay. I forgot you said you were linking up
with her today. Well, tell her I said hi. Don't want to
interrupt and kiss my princess for me," I told her.

"Aight, I tell her when she comes out the bathroom.
I'll see you later," she said before we disconnected the
call.

"Oh shit. Nigga, what the fuck you gonna do?" Zaire
asked.

"Well, you know damn well this is a done deal with
us. I don't play that cheating shit, I thought I left the
hoes alone when I met her ass, but I guess not. She
didn't have to do me like that. I fucking love that girl.
This is why I don't settle down with these bitches."

"Damn, bro. I'm really sorry. I thought she was a real
one," Zaire said. After venting to my brother a little
longer, I bounced. I wasn't sure how I was gonna
handle this, but what I did know was it was over, and
she wasn't taking my daughter a damn place.

*****

I decided to go straight home when I left Zaire's crib. Even though it was still early, I poured myself a shot and smoked a blunt and before I knew it my ass was knocked out on the couch. Hearing my princess crying caused me to wake up.

"Hey, daddy's princess. I see you finally made it back home. How was your day out with auntie?" I asked, knowing damn well she wasn't with her.

I wasn't about to play games with Tasha tonight, so I was ready to say what I needed to say and move on. Cheating was the one thing I didn't play around with. Now, if you single do you, but once you make that commitment, that's an entirely different story. I do too much freaky shit to her ass for me to share the pussy. So as much as I loved her, I had to end it. I got up, so I could go put Serenity in her playpen and grabbed the monitor. I didn't want her to see or hear me and Tasha arguing.

"Where's the baby?" Tasha asked.

"I put her in her playpen because I need to talk to you and didn't want her to be in here in case shit got loud. I'm not gonna sugarcoat shit. Tasha, the one thing I won't ever accept is being lied to and played. So as much as I love you, I can no longer be in a relationship with you. We gonna have to figure out this co-parent shit, "I told Tasha, seriously.

"Cameron, what the fuck are you talking about? Who's lying? You just gonna break up with me without telling me why?" She yelled.

"Keep your fucking voice down, and your hoe ass is the one that's lying. I know you weren't with Nyla today. I was at the house when I called you, and you told me that you were there. I was talking to Zaire and Nyla was in the kitchen cooking. I hate to be lied to. Also, know that you were with Brandon, so miss me with the bullshit and save your lies for a dumb ass nigga that will believe you," I snapped. I was about to snap and show her ass how rude a nigga could get. Tasha was standing there looking stupid as shit.

"Cameron, I'm sorry that I lied, but it's not what you think. Me and Brandon has never had sex since we've been together. I swear! Cameron, please don't do this to Serenity!" Tasha pleaded, but all that did was piss me off even more.

"Tasha, are you fucking kidding me right now!! Don't do this to Serenity? You did this shit! You broke up our family, not me. You're the one that's around here creeping with your best friend's brother, not me!" I yelled. "Then you had the nerve to say you haven't had sex with him since we've been together. So, you fucked that nigga before? You know what? Don't answer that because it doesn't even matter at this point. You're no longer my problem," I said dismissively.

"Cameron, I'm sorry. I didn't mean to hurt you, but I swear on our daughter that we didn't have sex," she argued. I wasn't trying to hear that shit because sex or no sex, it's still cheating.

"Tasha, it honestly doesn't matter if you fucked that nigga or not. It's still cheating. If you had to lie about who you were with, that mean you were doing something I wouldn't approve of. If you kissed that nigga, had oral with that nigga, it's still fucking cheating. I'm not talking to no bitches at all, not a single one. Now, I don't trust you, so we could never be together. I'm done with this conversation, you need to go," I yelled.

"So, you really going to put me and your daughter out in the streets?" Tasha cried. I looked at that bitch like she was crazy. Apparently, Tasha had lost her fucking mind.

"I'm putting you the fuck out; my daughter isn't going any damn where until you figure out where you gonna be staying and I make sure she's gonna be good. Until then, I need you to go," I told her. Tasha looked so heartbroken, but I didn't care. She shouldn't have tried to play me. I walked in the room to check on my daughter and she was knocked out. The thoughts of her taking my baby with her to meet up with him pissed me off even more.

Tasha went in the room to pack up some of my things and I sat in the living room waiting for her to get the fuck out of my sight. Her presence here was getting to me. A nigga was really hurting right now, but I had to stand my ground and do what I needed to do for me. I thought we had a good thing, but apparently, I wasn't enough for her. Tasha finally walked into the living room carrying two overnight bags.

"Cameron, I'm truly sorry. I love you and I don't want us to end." I didn't even bother to reply or look at her hoe ass. "And what about Serenity? I'm not going go a day without seeing my daughter, Cameron just because we are going through something," Tasha stated.

"I have no desire to keep you from our daughter, just call or text before you come. I don't want you to walk in on me and see me knee deep in some pussy," I told Tasha harshly. I knew that would get to her, but she needed to feel the hurt that I was feeling. Tears formed in her eyes and I put my head down.

"Wow, Cameron," was all Tasha said before walking out the door.

Chapter Twelve

Tasha

I couldn't believe what I got myself into. I lost a good man because I wanted to entertain the idea of someone I knew I couldn't be with. Now I was staying in a hotel while looking for a place. It's been three days since Cameron and I broke up. I still spent time and saw Serenity every day, but whenever I went to the house, Cameron would go in the room, so he didn't have to look at me. That shit was starting to eat at me bad. I didn't realize how much Cameron meant to me until this shit happened. I had one more thing to get out the way before things got even worse. I was on my way over to talk to Nyla before she heard it first from Cameron or Zaire. The last thing I needed was to be beefing with my best friend on top of dealing with my breakup.

Knowing Nyla, I knew she wouldn't be happy about me and Brandon, but I still felt like it was time to tell her about our history. When I got to the house, Nyla opened the door for me and we walked to the patio.

"Hey, bestie. Wassup with you and where is my Goddaughter?" Nyla asked with a big smile.

"She's with Cameron," I replied dryly.

"Tasha, what's going on? You don't seem like yourself," Nyla asked with a concerned voice.

"Nyla, I need to tell you something, and I know you won't be happy about it, but please just let me tell you the entire story before you flip out, I stated.

"Tasha, you're scaring me. Wassup?"

"I'm in love with Brandon. The night of my seventeenth birthday, Brandon took my virginity. We hooked up a few more times after that, but then we stopped because neither of us wanted to hurt you. And I've been in love with him ever since. Brandon is the love of my life. We haven't had sex since we were younger, but we've been spending a lot of time together and talking heavy since the night he broke up with Mariah.

The other day I went to meet up with him to tell him that I couldn't do this sneaking around thing anymore and that I was gonna work it out with Cameron. The problem is I told Cameron that me and the baby was with you all day. I was really with Brandon, and Cameron was here with y'all, so he knew I was lying, and he knew I was with Brandon. When I got home, Cameron put me out, and I've been staying in a hotel until I find somewhere to stay. He's keeping Serenity until I get on my feet," I cried. The first few seconds were awkward because it was so quiet all you could hear were my sniffles.

"Wow, that was an earful. So, you and my brother, huh? I can't trust anyone these days. Wow, Tasha. You and my brother? And when did you become a liar and a cheater, Tasha? How can we continue a friendship that's based off secrets and lies?" Nyla asked.

"Nyla, I'm sorry. I swear I wanted to tell you when it first happened, but I was scared to lose your friendship. I didn't plan to fall in love with him; it just happened. I can't afford to lose you, Nyla. You and my daughter is all I have," I cried. I really did feel bad about how this played out, but the truth was I couldn't help that my heart longed for Brandon. I tried to avoid Brandon to keep my feelings at bay, but once we started to see one another more, my feelings were in full force.

"Tasha, I honestly don't know what to say to you right now. Not only did you do something I asked you not to, but you had the nerve to do it and keep it from me for years. Then started creeping with him again, and the only reason you're telling me now is because you got caught by Cameron, and you knew I would find out at some point. How can I trust you after this? I'm madder at the fact that you kept this shit from then I actually am about you dealing with Brandon. I can't hold you. I can see why you fell for Brandon; my brother is handsome and well put together. Even as a teenager, he has always had his shit together. But what wasn't cool was for you to sneak around with him then smile in my face every day. That's why I'm so pissed the fuck off. Then to make matters worse, Brandon ass lying and keeping secrets too," Nyla stated. Nyla had every right to feel the way she was feeling. I guess I would feel the same way.

"You're right, Nyla, and I'm so sorry I never meant to hurt you. This secret has been eating me alive since I was seventeen. I lost my virginity and couldn't even tell you because it was your brother, so I had to make you believe that Seth was my first. And every guy I dated after that I was looking for Brandon in them, and they didn't compare. And the only one that came close was Cameron, and I fucked that up," I told her honestly with a shoulder shrug.

"Look, Tasha, I'm pissed, but you need a friend right now, so I'm gonna put my feelings behind me for now. You and my God daughter can stay here until you find a place," Nyla stated. I looked at her like she was crazy. That would be so awkward to stay here.

"Don't you think that would be a little awkward with being here with you and Zaire? I mean, I cheated on his brother. Do you think he would want me here?" I asked.

"You let me worry about my husband. I can handle him," she stated. "There's no point in paying for a room every day when I have space for you to stay here. But you owe me a favor, let's go pay Brandon a little visit, I'm about to make him real uncomfortable," she stated with a devilish grin.

"Nyla, I don't think that's a good idea. He has no idea I told you about us; he doesn't know that Cameron and I broke up. We haven't talked since that day. He wasn't exactly happy with me ending whatever that was that we had."

"That's even better. Besides, bitch, you owe me," Nyla said. I just shook my head. Nyla picked up her cell and called Brandon to see if he was home, and he was, so we headed over to his crib. When we got to Brandon's house, he looked surprised to see me. Brandon was looking good as shit that nigga answered the door with no shirt and some baller shorts.

"Wassup with y'all? What brings y'all by?" Brandon asked.

"Do I need a reason to come see my one and only brother? But I did have something I wanted to talk to you about. So, you've been single for a few months now, don't you think you should get back out there? It's this girl that I want you to meet that I think would be perfect for you. She's single, pretty, light skin and thick, just like you like them," Nyla said. And although I knew she wasn't serious, it still made me feel some type of way for some reason.

"Nyla, when the hell did you become a matchmaker? But I'm good. I'm just gonna chill for a little bit longer. But thanks for your concern," he told her while cutting his eye at me. I quickly put my head down.

"I just want my brother to be happy, I mean, I thought Mariah was the one, but obviously she was just a cheating whore. I guess you're going to be upset with me, but you might wanna put some clothes on because she's on her way here right now as we speak," Nyla stated. Brandon's eyes got wide as hell.

"Nyla, why the hell would you do something like that? I don't do blind dates, and I damn sure don't do strangers coming to my house. You need to tell her not to come," Brandon told her. I wasn't sure exactly what Nyla's plan was, but it was kinda funny watching Brandon's reactions.

"Too late, bro. She's pulling up now," she stated, and Brandon huffed and puffed. He wasn't too happy with Nyla right now.

"I'm going to kill you, Nyla. This shit wasn't cool at all," Brandon said while going to put some clothes on. Brandon came back out wearing a shirt and some jeans. Although it was a basic outfit, Brandon was looking good as hell.

"Aight, where is she? But just so you know, I'm not going out with her. I'm not looking to date right now," he told Nyla. Nyla just smirked before speaking.

"Well, bro, that's gonna be your loss. She's a really great girl, and she's your type, but if you don't want to date her, that's cool. Brandon, meet my best friend Tasha. This is my brother Brandon, and I think y'all would be perfect for one another," Nyla said, shocking the hell out of me.

Was Nyla giving me her blessing to be with Brandon? I was beyond shocked, and Brandon looked more confused than anything.

"Nyla, what the hell type of games you playing?" Brandon asked in confusion.

"I'm not playing, apparently you wanted to be with her bad enough to lie and keep secrets from me for so many years. And then was sneaking around with her while she was in a relationship. Well, sneaking around with you caused her relationship to end. So, are you sure you don't want to date her?" Nyla asked.

"Damn, so you know, huh. I'm sorry, Nyla. I just didn't want to hurt you or break up y'all friendship. I've been in love with Tasha for years, but I decided to put your feelings first. I never wanted to keep this away from you. Do you forgive me, lil sis?" Brandon replied.

"I think I need a little more convincing, so maybe lunch tomorrow would help smooth it over," Nyla shot back and the three of us just laughed it off.

"But for now, I have to go sweet talk my husband, and get your room together. I think the two of you need to talk. I'll pick you up in a few hours and take you get your belongings from Cameron's," Nyla said to me before heading out the door. I just nodded. I truly loved my best friend. I fucked with her the long way.

Chapter Thirteen

Nyla

"Hey, baby. Wassup, what do you want to talk about? Is everything good?" Zaire asked.

"Yes, baby, I'm good. I'm not sure if you heard already, but Cameron and Tasha broke up a few days ago. I don't want this to come in between you and Cameron, but Tasha needs a place to stay until she finds her own place," I said to Zaire while rubbing his shoulders.

"Yeah, I heard, and I figured she would be staying here. She's good, I don't get involved in other people's business. Tasha good with me. I mean, she didn't have to do that to my brother like that. He actually loves her ass, which is a first."

"Yeah, that shit wasn't cool at all, and you know I wasn't happy about it being with my brother even though they didn't fuck it was still wrong of her. But she's grown. The only relationship I'm worried about is ours," I told my husband, placing a kiss on his lips.

"That's the only relationship that matters, but you better stop kissing and rubbing on me like you doing before you get fucked," Zaire threatened. I was down for that, so I decided to get the party started.

"Well, what if I want to be fucked?" I flirted, and Zaire didn't waste any time pulling my pants down, bending me over the couch, and giving me the business.

In spite of everything that has taken place, Zaire and I were actually doing great. I was so happy that I decided to give us a chance and work through our marriage. Zaire was everything that you could ask for in a man. Sometimes he was a little too good to be true, but I was loving every moment of it. Once me and Zaire finished sexing, I washed off so I could go get the room ready for Tasha and Serenity. I wasn't happy with the situation with Tasha, Cameron, and my brother, but I understood. I just think that Tasha should have handled the situation a little better because all she did was fuck Cameron over and that I didn't like. I was sure that things would be a little awkward for a while between all of us, but hopefully, we would be able to get past it as a family.

"Babe, I'm going over to Cameron's for a minute because I know he needs me right now. Plus, I want to be the one to tell him that Tasha will be staying with us. Are you cooking tonight, or do you want to eat out?" Zaire stated.

"You can grab something I don't really feel cooking," I answered.

A few hours later, I was on my way to pick up Tasha up from the hotel she was staying at. She texted me a while ago to tell me that she was back there. When I pulled up, she was waiting outside. We got to Cameron's house in no time. I debated if I wanted to go in or not because I knew there would be tension, and I didn't feel like dealing with that shit tonight. We got out of the car, rang the bell, and Zaire opened the door and let us in. Camron wasn't anywhere in sight. Tasha walked upstairs, and I stood downstairs with Zaire.

"Let me know if you need my help with anything," I told her.

"So, how is Cameron holding up? Was he okay with her staying with us?"

"He's good, and he said he didn't give a shit where she stayed as long as his daughter was safe," Zaire answered. Did you decide what you want to eat for dinner?" My husband asked.

"It doesn't matter to me. I just know that I'm hungry, do you have a taste for anything particular?"

"Besides you, nah, nothing else comes to mind, " Zaire flirted, causing me to blush. I swear he always knows what to say to keep a smile on my face. Tasha walked downstairs with some of her belongings, and Cameron was right behind her carrying the baby.

"Hey, sis. Wassup?"

"Hey, bro. I'm good, how are you?"

"I've never been better. Look, sis, I don't have any beef with you, but I do have a few choice words for your brother when I see him," Cameron stated.

"Y'all are two grown men that can both handle y'all own, so do you, bro," I told him honestly. I mean, I don't blame him for wanting to say something. I'm disappointed that my brother would do that to another nigga when Mariah just did the same shit to him. It didn't take us long to move Tasha's belongings out. I took the baby to the car to give Tasha and Cameron a little privacy.

*****

"Baby, where are you taking me, and why do I have to be blindfolded?" I asked Zaire as he drove.

"I told you that I have a big surprise for you, just relax. We'll be there in just a few more minutes," he said. I couldn't wait to see what the surprise was, but I was sure I would like it because Zaire hasn't felled me thus far plus I was easy to please. The car came to a stop, and I couldn't help but get excited.

"Okay, we're here, but don't take the blindfold off yet," he told me.

Zaire got out of the car and helped me get out since I couldn't see. We walked a few steps before we stopped moving. I felt Zaire removing my blindfold, and when I opened my eyes, we were standing in front of a building. At first, I was sure what the hell I was looking at, I guess I was so excited that I was even paying attention. The sign read, *Nyla's safe haven.*"

"Baby, what is this?" I asked.

"It's your mentoring spot for sexually assaulted teens and women. Buying you this building was the least I could do. I love you, Nyla baby. I think you're gonna do great things here," Zaire explained. All I could do was cry. I couldn't believe he brought me a building for my mentoring program I wanted to open. We had that conversation when we first met.

"Oh my God, Zaire. I can't believe you did this. Thank you so much," I cried.

"I'll do anything for you, Mrs. Price. Now, let's go take a look inside," he said, passing me the keys. When I opened the door, the place was nice and spacious. My mind started thinking of the great things I could do to this building. I was so grateful for Zaire. I walked around to look at the building, and I loved it. I walked over to Zaire and stood in front of him.

"Thank you so much, baby," I said to Zaire, placing a kiss on his lips. I dropped to my knees, unbuckled his pants, freed his thickness, and swallowed him whole. I slurped on his thickness nice and slow until it began to swell up in my mouth. Once Zaire was nice and hard, I started sucking him fast and sloppily.

"Fuck, baby! This shit feels good," Zaire groaned while palming my head. I took him from out of my mouth and began to slowly lick the tip, teasing him before sucking again. Minutes later, my husband's seeds filled my mouth. I swallowed every drop, then licked my lips. When I stood up, Zaire picked me up, hiked up my dress, removed my panties to the side, and slid into my wetness. Zaire stroked slowly as I rested my head on the wall, enjoying my husband's thickness, filling up my insides.

"Oh fuck, Zaire!" I cooed. Zaire's strokes became faster and I felt myself about to cum.

"You ready to cum for me, Mrs. Price?" Zaire asked through gritted teeth as he slid in and out of me at a fast pace.

"Yes, baby! I'm about to cum!" I yelled loudly, hearing my sex sounds echo throughout the empty building.

"Fuck! I'm right behind you," Zaire groaned as he emptied his seeds inside me. Panting to catch my breath, Zaire slowly put me down so I can stand. I reached in my purse to grab a wipe so I could wipe me and Zaire off before further touring the rest of the building. "Damn girl, that head game of yours is vicious," Zaire said, licking his lips.

"That's just a preview of what you're going to get later tonight," I replied with a sexy smile, before walking off and leaving him standing there to ponder.

After leaving my new building, we went to grab a bite to eat. We decided to go to Longhorn Steakhouse. I couldn't wait to eat because my ass was starving. I ordered the pork chops with mashed potatoes and corn, and Zaire ordered the steak and the same sides as me.

"So, Mrs. Price, what exactly do you plan to do now that you have your building? What are your next steps?" Zaire asked, breaking me from my .

"Honestly, baby, I don't know where to begin. First, I have to put my own touches on the building. Maybe hire a few people to help out like a therapist or something. Baby, I don't know, but I'll figure it out."

"We'll figure it out, together" Zaire said. We finished our food and headed out the door. On the way to the car, my husband smacked my ass.

"Is that Zeek?" A familiar voice asked. I knew that voice from anywhere. My hands started to shake, and I dropped my food on the ground. When I looked up to confirm what I already knew, I was looking into the face of the man that raped me. It was the man that slipped something in my drink, the man that forced Zaire to rape me. Why the fuck was this happening to me? The more I tried to get away from my past, the more it was thrown in my face. I guess Zaire could see how scared I was, so he stepped in front of me and grabbed my hand.

"It's you," I said to the guy, and he looked at me like I was crazy. "You ruined my life! I shouted, causing a scene as I trembled.

"Baby, calm down. Let me handle this, go to the car," Zaire turned and said, but I refused to move.

"Bishop, we need to talk," Zaire stated.

"Zeek, what's this about? And I go by Pastor Lewis now. That's right, I turned my life around. I have my own church and everything," the man said.

"How do you sleep at night after what you did to me?" I asked angrily.

"I have never seen you a day in my life. I think you have me confused with someone else," he said, pissing me off.

"I'll never confuse the man that brutally raped me and made others rape me, You ruined my life!" I yelled angrily as the tears fell from my face.

"I don't appreciate your false accusations young lady, I am a man of God," he shot back.

"Bishop, look, we need to talk. I'm sure you don't want to do this right here in front of everyone," Zaire stated.

"I told you, it's Pastor Lewis now and again, I don't know this young lady."

"Sweetie, who are these people?" The woman that was with him asked.

"This young man and I used to be friends, but this woman has me confused with someone else," he said. I stepped in front of Zaire, going from being scared to being angry and bitter.

"I am the woman that you brutally raped. Now you can pretend you don't know me, but if you don't, you will remember me real soon. I am going to ruin you like you ruined my life, Pastor Lewis. Come on, baby. I'm ready to go," I stated then walked off. I wasn't sure what came over me, but I was full of anger, and I planned to seek revenge. The only reason I didn't call the cops is because I wanted him to suffer first.

"Baby, are you okay?" Zaire asked.

"I'm just fine, but he will feel my wrath," I stated before getting in the car.

"Look, I don't know what happened to you back there, but I didn't even recognize who you were. It was sexy and scary at the same time, but I need to ask what exactly you plan to do?"

"I haven't figured it out yet. Just know he's gonna pay," I replied.

"Just don't do anything without me, Nyla. Promise me?" he said.

"I promise but just know that whatever I decide rather you agree or not, I'm going to do it. So, you need to promise that you will let me handle this," I answered Zaire. Zaire just looked at me for a few moments before speaking.

"Nyla, you're starting to scare me. I know that you're hurt, and I want him to pay just as much as you do, but I want you to think about this rationally."

"Can we just leave this conversation alone for now? I don't want to talk about him right now," I said, dismissing the conversation altogether.

Zaire didn't say anything else and the ride home was quiet. The entire ride I thought about what just took place. I couldn't believe that he said he was a pastor now. How could he rest his head so peacefully at night after what he's done to me? He don't look like he lost a night's sleep.

When we got home, Cameron was at the house picking up Serenity for the weekend. I wasn't sure what these feelings were that I was feeling, but my emotions were starting to get the best of me. I could feel the tears filling up in my eyes. Before I knew it, I started shaking and crying.

"Nyla, what's wrong? What happened? Why are you crying?" Tasha asked, getting the attention of Zaire and Cameron.

"I saw the man that raped me. I swear I'm gonna ruin him. I swear I am, just watch," I said repeatedly.

"Oh my God, Nyla," Tasha hugged me tightly as I cried hard on her shoulder. As much as I tried to hold in my cries, the harder I cried. It was like I realized something within that I didn't even know I had inside of me. Tasha just rubbed my back as I cried. Zaire just stood there and I think he knew that I needed my best friend right now. After I calmed down and stopped crying, I told Tasha everything that happened when I saw that piece of shit. Of course, she had a lot to say and was down for whatever I was down for. The problem was I wasn't sure what my plan was. I just knew that he needed to be dealt with.

Chapter Fourteen

Zaire

It's been two weeks since I ran into that nigga Bishop and I couldn't believe that he popped out of nowhere. I had a private detective looking for his ass for a few months, and it was like that nigga just vanished, but now he's here. I hit up Brandon so we could figure out how we wanted to move. I was keeping up with this tho'. I found out where is the church, I even now knew where that nigga laid his head at. It turned out that the woman he was with was his wife. I really wanted to have a conversation with that nigga before I make a move. I at least wanted to give him a chance to try to right his wrongs. I wondered if he truly didn't remember what he did or was he putting on a front for his wife. Ever since that day, Nyla hasn't been the same. She has been like a sassy bad ass chick. It was kind of a turn-on but a little scary at the same time. I knew she had something up her sleeve that she wasn't telling me, so I knew I had to be on her ass. With my niece being around every day it was making me want a baby, but every time I mentioned it to Nyla, she would always say that she wasn't ready. I understood to degree, but I wanted to at least have two kids. It didn't matter what sex, so I wanted to get a start on them.

"Hey, baby. What you doing?" Nyla asked.

"Not much, just thinking about some shit," I answered.

"Is everything okay?"

"Everything is great," I told her.

"So, I've been thinking since so much shit has been going on, I thought maybe we should start going to church," Nyla replied, and I looked at her ass like she was crazy. It wasn't that I had anything against church, I just knew that it was more to it than what she was saying. I decided to play along for now to see what she was up to.

"I wasn't expecting that, but okay. Do you have a church in mind? And when would you like to start?" I asked.

"We can start Sunday, and I haven't decided what church yet. I'm still looking online," Nyla said, but I didn't believe her.

"Aight well, let me know what church you decide on," I told her.

Nyla kissed me while skipping off happily like I just agreed to take her on vacation. I knew she was up to no good. I just had to find out what the hell it was. I was sitting in my office going through my emails. I was leaving the record label to open up my own lounge. I planned to have the grand opening in a few months. The guy that was doing my sign just emailed me a picture of it, and I was feeling it. I decided to call it *Symphony*. I would still write songs for people, but I didn't want to run the company anymore.

A couple of hours later, I decided to pay my mom a visit. I haven't seen her for like two weeks. When I got there, my mom answered the door, but she didn't look too happy to see me.

"Hey, mom. Wassup, you good?" I asked. I was looking at her appearance, and something was wrong.

"I'm fine, Zaire. What brings you by?" she asked me.

"Mom, are you sure you're good? You don't look too hot," I told her honestly. Something was off with the way my mom was looking. I just couldn't figure out what it was. I couldn't tell whether she looked like she was getting high again or sick.

"Yes, Zaire. I'm good, baby, how are you?"

"I'm good, mom. I just came to check on my favorite lady since I haven't seen you in a couple of weeks."

"How's my daughter?" my mom asked.

"She's good, just getting her mentoring program together."

"That's good to hear,baby. I'm glad that she's opening a place for rape victims to come share what they went through and get some therapy without being judged. You got yourself a really great woman. You bet not fuck it up with her, Zaire," my mom complimented.

"I promise I won't fuck it up. I couldn't picture my life without her," I told my mom honestly. Nyla meant everything to me. I never knew you could love someone the way I love her.

"Where's Charles?"

"He's at work? He should be home shortly."

I sat and talked with my mom a little longer before heading home to my wife. The entire ride home all I could think about was my mom. Something was off with her. Tomorrow I planned to call Cameron and my aunt Pat to see if they have seen her or talked to her lately and if they did what were their thoughts.

*****

It's been two days since the day I went to see my mom, and it was weighing heavy on me. Cameron, my aunt Pat and myself were on my way over to my moms so they could tell me if I was tripping or not. When we got to my mom's, I knocked on the door, and Charles answered the door.

"Hey, y'all. Is everything okay? We weren't expecting any company today," Charles stated, and for some reason, I found his statement a little odd.

"Yeah, we good. Where's my mom?" Cameron shot back sarcastically. My mom walked into the living room with a robe and scarf on looking like she was just getting up. I looked at her then at my watch and it was definitely too early to be in bed.

"Hey, what are y'all doing here? Is everything okay?" She asked in a concerned tone while wiping the crust from her eyes.

"Yeah, mom. We're good, but what the hell is going on with you? And please don't tell me nothing. We're not leaving until you tell us what the hell is going on," I replied.

"Zaire, I don't know what the hell you're talking about. I know the only reason y'all here is because of you. I don't know what you told them, but I'm good. Can't even get no damn sleep in my own damn house," she said angrily.

"Mom, cut the shit what's going on with you?" Cameron chimed in. The room fell silent, and my mom just stood there as tears filled her eyes.

"Come sit down," she stated, and we did as we were told. As soon as we sat down, Charles walked over, sat on the other side of my mom, and grabbed her hand. "Look, there's no easy way for me to say this, but I just found out that I have cancer. It's pretty far gone. They said they're gonna do all they can, but it's not looking too good," she stated, and I swear in that moment my heart stopped beating.

"Mom, what are you saying?" I asked.

"I'm saying that I may not have much longer to live. They are waiting on one more test to determine what my options are."

"Are you trying to tell me that you might die?" I asked, praying that wasn't what she was trying to say.

"Yes, Zaire, that's exactly what I'm trying to say," my mom answered. Her answer stung like hell, and I let out a long scream that I couldn't control. I saw the tears in my Aunt Pat's eyes, and when I looked at Cameron, he was wearing a blank expression.

"Nah, fuck that," Cameron mumbled before getting up and walking out the front door. I was about to go after him, but my mom stopped me.

"Let him be, Zaire. He'll come back in; he just needs some air. I know what I told y'all came as a shock. I'm shocked myself. I was trying to wait for the results for the last test before I said anything," my mom cried, and that shit broke a nigga's heart.

"Nah, I don't accept that! This bullshit!" I yelled.

"Zaire, honey, calm down. I know this is a hard thing to hear and accept, but prayer is the only way to deal with this because no matter what the doctors say, God has the final say so," my Aunt Pat said. I heard what she was saying, but the thought of losing my mom was killing a nigga inside. I wasn't the type of nigga that could hide my feelings. I was more on the sensitive side and wore my emotions on my sleeve. Cameron, however, was different from me. He handled everything angrily.

Cameron finally walked back in the house and joined us back on the couch. I could tell that he was crying, and I could definitely relate to how he was feeling. Just the thought of my mom dying was making me sick to my stomach. I feel like I just got her back in my life, and they trying to say I may lose her. My mom was doing so good. She stopped doing drugs, got a job, and found herself a good husband. Why would God take my mother away as soon as she got her shit together? I couldn't bear to stay another minute, so I said my goodbyes and bounced.

The car ride home was silent. I didn't even want to hear music; the only thing I could hear was the thoughts that were running through my head. The tears slowly ran down my face as the thought of me losing my mom to cancer filled my head. I was at a stop sign, but I just sat there at the sign and banged my hands on the steering wheel. The car behind me was beeping their horn at me. I stopped banging on the steering wheel and pulled off. When I walked in the house, Nyla and Tasha were in the living room watching Tv.

"Hey, baby. How was your visit with your mom?" Nyla asked when I walked in. For some reason, her question made the tears come down harder. And before I knew it, I was crying hard and loud. Nyla jumped up and ran over to me. "Baby, what's wrong? What happened?" She asked in a worried tone.

"She has cancer, baby. She said it's not looking good, and she may not have long to live. They're waiting on her test results to determine what the next step is," I cried.

"Oh my God, baby. I'm so sorry," Nyla said while hugging me. I just laid on her shoulders and cried. I needed Nyla more than anything right now. If I was acting like this just at the thought, I could only imagine how I would feel if something really happened to her. I finally had gotten myself together thanks to my wife's kind words. Now I was hungry as a hostage.

While Nyla was in the kitchen making dinner, I decided to call and check on my brother, but he didn't answer the phone. I knew he was probably fucked up in the head right now. I wish I could be there for him the way I wanted to be, but the truth was I was fucked up right now and needed someone to be there for me. After dinner, I took a shower and made love to my wife for damn near two hours before finally going to sleep.

Chapter Fifteen

Cameron

After I left my mom's house, I was so fucked up in the head that all I could do was cry the entire ride home. I knew me and my mom didn't see eye to eye all the time, but I loved my mom so much, and the thought of losing her was really fucking with a nigga. I wasn't the type of man that cried, but I cried enough tonight to make up for a lifetime worth of crying. I needed to take my mind off this shit just for tonight. I poured myself a drink and lit a blunt. I heard somebody knocking on the door and I knew it was nobody but Zaire or Brian. When I opened the door, I was shocked to see Tasha standing there with my daughter. I stepped to the side and let her in. Serenity was knocked out, so I took her from Tasha's arm and laid her in her room. When I walked back to the living room, Tasha was just standing there. I wasn't sure what the hell she was doing there. She was just standing there looking at me like I was crazy.

"Wassup, Tasha? What you doing here?" I asked.

"I heard about your mom and I'm really sorry, Cameron. I hope everything works out for her. I came over because I thought you could use some company. I hope you don't mind that I came by to check on you," Tasha said sympathetically.

I had mixed feelings about Tasha being here since she did break my heart a few months ago. But oddly, I was kinda glad that she came by. I couldn't lie and say that Tasha didn't have my heart, but I was played for some corny ass Brandon. I mean, I wasn't no hating ass nigga. Brandon was a cool dude in my eyes until he starting sneaking around with my girl. But even then, he didn't have shit on me.

"Yeah, a nigga fucked up over my mom having cancer, but I'm kinda glad that you came. Well, I'm more surprised than anything. I thought you would be somewhere with your little boyfriend," I shot back.

"Cameron, I don't have a boyfriend. I'm simply here to check up on my daughter's father and the man I love in his time of need," she replied, catching me off guard.

I didn't think she still loved me to be honest. But I wasn't about to feed into what she said.

"Well, thanks. I truly appreciate you for coming through and checking up on me because I could use the company," I told her honestly.

"Anytime, Cameron. Do you want to talk about it?"

"Nah, not right now. I just want to chill. If anything, I need a distraction from it," I replied.

"Well, a distraction is what you will get. Let me go make something to eat because I know you haven't eaten yet," she said, sashaying to the kitchen. I just shook my head. I had to admit my baby momma was bad as shit. I was about to say something slick to her, but she was saved by the cries of Serenity. I went and picked my daughter up, and as soon as she saw my face, she started smiling.

"Hey, daddy's princess. I missed you so much, do you want to stay with daddy tonight?" I cooed.

She wiggled her cute little body like she understood what I was saying. After changing her diaper, I went to grab a bottle. I knew she was hungry because she always did some weird thing with her lip when she was ready to eat. After she was fed and burped, Tasha brought me my plate. She made some spaghetti with Italian sausage. I missed her being around.

After eating dinner, I sat and talked with Tasha for a bit more, and before I knew it, my tongue was in her mouth. The light moaning made my dick hard as a brick. I pulled her shirt over her head and started sucking on her nipples while unfastening her jeans. Once I had Tasha naked, the only thing I wanted to do was feel Tasha's insides. I didn't waste any time putting this dick into Tasha's wetness. I started stroking at a slow pace then sped up. Tasha started throwing all that ass up, and that shit drove me crazy.

"Fuck! This pussy feels so fucking good!" I groaned while pounding the fuck out of her. I swear Tasha pussy was feeling so good.

"Oh my God, Cameron! I miss this dick so fucking much," Tasha moaned loudly. Her words, for some reason, triggered me, and I blacked out.

"Oh, you miss this dick? Then why the fuck did you start fucking with that corny nigga then?" I asked through gritted teeth. I sped up my strokes and went deeper and harder. I bet that nigga ain't never fuck you like this, did he?" I asked, grabbing her hair.

"I'm gonna make you regret leaving this dick," I groaned.

"Oh fuck, Cameron! I'm sorry for what I did. I don't want nobody's dick but yours, I swear. I love this dick!" she yelled while cumming hard. I heard my daughter crying, but I couldn't stop fucking Tasha until I bust. After a few more strokes, I came hard as hell.

"Ahhhh, fuck! a nigga about to cum!" I groaned loudly, busting on Tasha's ass. I wasn't about to risk busting inside of her and catching something. I pulled out slowly and caught my breath so we could tend to my daughter.

I wiped off and went to get my daughter. As soon as I picked her up, she stopped crying and started smiling. I didn't even know it was possible to love someone the way that I loved my daughter. As I sat there with her, I thought about what just went down with me and Tasha. I knew that I still loved Tasha, but I just don't think that I would ever be able to trust her again after what she had done. I mean, if she wasn't feeling me anymore, then I could have dealt with that. But sneaking around on me with my sister in-law's brother was just disrespectful, messy, and distasteful. I don't know if I just slept with her because I missed her or because I was going through something. One way or another, I shouldn't have done it.

Tasha walked into the baby's nursery, and we locked eyes. It wasn't until that moment that I realized how hurt I was, and I needed answers. Tasha and I haven't been together in a few months, but I refused to talk about it. If it wasn't about my daughter, then we weren't talking.

"Tasha, why did you do me like that? Why did you fuck around on me?" I asked. Tasha looked like she was thrown off by my question. She sat down and put her head down.

"Cameron, are you sure you want to talk about this right now with everything that's going on?" she asked.

"Yeah, I'm good, so why did you do it?"

"Honestly, Cameron, I know what I did was wrong, but when I said I didn't sleep with Brandon, I was telling the truth. Yes, I was meeting up with him and spending time with him, but that was as far as it went. If I could be honest, the day I lied about being at Nyla's, I went to meet with him to completely break everything off. I love you, Cameron. I swear I do," Tasha stated.

"Do you love him and how long has it been since you fucked him?" I asked. I wasn't sure why I cared if she still loved him at this point, but I wanted to know.

"I'm going to be honest with you. Brandon was my first, I haven't had sex with him since I was seventeen. I would be lying to you right now if I told you that I didn't have feelings for Brandon. I always felt like I was in love with him and wanted to be with him, but we never got together because of Nyla. After being with you then losing you made me realize that I didn't want to be without you. I knew I loved you, but it took for me to lose you to realize that I was in love with you. I want to be with you, Cameron. I want my family back. I want you. Not being with you has been one of the hardest things I had to deal with," Tasha admitted. I didn't know what to say to her. Something in my heart told me she was being honest about what went down with her and Brandon. I even believed her when she said that she was in love with me.

"Look, Tasha, I have to keep it real with you. I don't know if I could trust you again. I love you too, but I just need some time to think about all of this. It's a lot going on and a lot of shit that has happened within the last few months that has a nigga fucked up in the head. I'm not saying no to us trying to work it, but I am saying not at this moment. I need to take my time with this, and you need to make sure that you don't have any type of romantic feelings for your little punk ass high school crush. Which by the way, I still plan to see him about that bitch nigga shit he did," I told her honestly. Tasha didn't respond right away. I could tell that her feelings was hurt, but I had to be honest with her.

"I understand, Cameron. I didn't think that if we did get together that it would be like tonight. I know we just had sex, but I'm smart enough to know that you only did it because you were in your feelings about your mom. I don't know if you have any regrets, but even if you do, I don't. But it's getting late, so I better get going," she replied.

"Tasha, why don't y'all just spend the night?" I said against my better judgment. I knew I didn't want to be with her, but I also didn't want her to leave tonight. I know I was probably being selfish, but I wanted what I wanted.

"Are you sure?"

"Yeah, I'm sure, but only if that's what you want to do." Tasha just nodded her head, yes.

I was happy as hell that she agreed to stay with me. I was just trying to hide my excitement. I didn't want to seem too excited. After about an hour passed, I gave my princess a bath and put her to bed. Once Serenity

174

was asleep. I took a shower and joined Tasha in the bedroom so I could put her ass to sleep. I knew we shouldn't have been fucking the way we were, but Tasha had some bomb ass pussy, and I was just the man to dig all up in that good wet wet.

Chapter Sixteen

Brandon

"You had no business fucking that girl anyway, Brandon. You knew how Nyla felt about that. Y'all crossed the line," Ariel said like she was my fucking mom.

"You know what, Ariel? You always got something to say about what everybody else is doing, but keep your fucking life private. How the hell do you or Nyla have the right to tell me who the hell I should date because of y'all feelings? Did anyone tell you that a woman eating another woman's pussy ain't normal?" I yelled at my sister, sick of her shit.

I knew I was hitting below the belt. I've always tried to protect my sisters and make sure they were good, but now I was tired, and they were grown. I could tell that Ariel was shocked and hurt at the things I said to her, but it was the truth, and it needed to be said.

"Wow, I never thought I see the day that you talk to me like that," she said, sounding wounded.

"Well, I never thought I would see the day when my sister would be such a judgmental bitch!" I yelled, regretting that I said it as soon as the words left my mouth. I felt like shit for calling my sister a bitch. A tear fell from her eyes and I knew that I had fucked up.

"Fuck you, Brandon," Ariel yelled, running out the door, and that made me feel even worse. But I wasn't going to chase after her because it was nothing at that moment that I could say to change what I said.

I had been blowing Tasha's phone up all night long but couldn't reach her. Just a couple of months ago, we were kicking it hot and heavy. The only thing we weren't doing was fucking, but we were definitely having oral sex and kissing. I knew I was wrong for sneaking around with Tasha while she had a man, especially since Mariah had just done the same shit to me. Finding out that Mariah cheated on me fucked me up in the head, but nothing shattered my heart more than finding out that Kavon wasn't my son. Since that day, I had a cold place in my heart, and the only one I really want to fuck with was Tasha. We were hanging tight until we met up, and she decided to work shit out with Cameron. I couldn't be but so mad, but that shit did sting a bit.

I damn near hated Mariah for what she did to me. I'm such a great guy, but maybe that's the problem. As crazy as it sounds, although I still had feelings for Tasha and could see myself with her, she's actually more of my best friend and that I could appreciate. Ironically after Nyla found out about me and Tasha and pretty much gave us permission to be together, we decided to just be friends. If we ended up together, then that's what it would be.

Nyla called me and said she wanted to go to church this Sunday. I knew she was up to know good, especially once Zaire told me about their run-in with that dude that raped her. I knew my sister and I was ready to bet my life that her ass was about to have us sitting up in that nigga's church. Ever since she ran into him, she's been different, but I liked it. Nyla always had a smart mouth, but now she was much tougher. The only way Nyla wasn't gonna completely get past her attack until she faced her attacker. So, whatever my sister had planned for that bastard, I had her back. My doorbell ringing brought me from my thoughts. I wasn't expecting anybody, so I didn't know who it could be. When I opened the door, I was shocked to see Cameron standing on the other side of my door.

"Listen, I need to holler at you. It will only take a minute," Cameron stated.

"Wassup?" I said.

"Listen, I know you and Tasha have history, and that's cool and all, but that shit y'all pulled a few months ago was foul as shit. Real niggas play by the code. I was sure that when I saw you, I was gonna want to throw my hands, but I ain't on that shit no more. I'm about to work shit out with Tasha, so I'm coming to you as a man to ask you to have some respect because I don't want to have to get reckless. We fam, my nigga, but that shit will fly out the window if you cross me after this conversation," Cameron stated, not holding any punches.

"You're right, I had no business sneaking around with Tasha while that was your girl. And I did break the code. That's' my bad, and as a man, I apologize. I respect you coming to me and talking about it like a man. And when it comes to me and Tasha, we just friends and I didn't want to disrespect y'all relationship. But I can't promise that if y'all don't work out that I won't make her mine," I replied.

"If it doesn't work out, you can do what you want. Just don't think my daughter is ever gonna call you daddy," Cameron shot back sarcastically.

"Deal. Anything else?"

"Nah, that's all I got to say," he stated before walking off. I had no choice but to respect Cameron. I honestly think he's good for her to be honest, but I won't share that with anyone but y'all. They say that Cameron and Zaire ain't from the street, but the way those two act, they seem like former drug dealers. Especially Cameron's ass.

I guess him and Tasha getting back together is probably why I haven't heard from her in a few days, but it was all good. Tasha and I had already decided to just be friends. I don't know if sneaking around was getting us off because when we were able to do it, we still didn't. My best friend Joey and Zaire were on their way over to chill for a bit.

I fucked with Zaire heavy. He was a real solid guy with a mixture of calm and crazy. He reminded me of myself a little. Thoughts of me and my sister arguing filled my head and I hated when we got into it. I loved Nyla and Ariel to death. I tried to call her, but of course, she didn't answer the phone, so I just hung up. I would give her a few days to calm down. I went in the kitchen to whip up some wings and fries for me and the fellas to eat. They should be here in about an hour. While cooking, I thought about getting back in the dating game because I didn't like being single. I was ready to settle down, do a little traveling and then have a couple kids. I thought I was gonna do that with Mariah, but we see how that went.

Chapter Seventeen

Nyla

I was in the mirror making sure I looked the part so I could head out to church. Today's church service is gonna be a service that no one will ever forget. Ever since the day me and Zaire ran into the man that ruined a part of me, I've been on a thousand. My attitude and demeanor was different. I wasn't the same softy anymore. The only way to get over this was to confront my attacker. I know people think I'm crazy for staying married to my husband, but I'm not. Now, if he wanted to do it or even enjoyed it, then I wouldn't have been able to. I asked everyone to go to church with me for support.

It's been a few weeks now since I planned to make my appearance to visit his church, I didn't tell anyone that it was his church or what I planned to do. I'm sure they weren't stupid and knew that I was up to something. I gave myself a once over, and I was satisfied with my look, I decided to look like a little southern bell. According to his Facebook page, today was his 2nd pastoral anniversary. Zaire walked in the room, and when I turned around, I swear I came on myself. I swear my husband was fine as hell, he was rocking a navy-blue Armani suit with a white shirt and a blue, white and yellow tie with gold cufflinks and jewelry. If I wasn't so anxious to get to church, I swear I would have fucked the shit out of his yellow ass.

"Hey, babe. Are you ready?" he asked, walking up behind me. The fragrance of his cologne drove me crazy. I turned around and answered him with a passionate kiss.

"I was ready, but after seeing and smelling you, I want some dick before we leave. But you have to be quick because I don't want to be late," I told him seductively. Zaire didn't waste no time hiking up my skirt, pulling my panties down, bending me over the dresser and inserting his thickness inside of me. After both of us came, Zaire went into the bathroom, came back with a soapy rag, and wiped me off.

"Was that quick enough?" Zaire asked with a sly smile.

"That was perfect. Now, let's get going," I told him, placing a kiss on his lips. We pulled up to the church in about twenty minutes. I took a deep breath before getting out the car. Zaire grabbed my hand and rubbed the back of it.

"Nyla, I'm not sure what you are up to, but I know this is Bishop's church. I won't ask what your plan is, just know that I got you no matter what," Zaire assured me. I knew he would know that I was up to something, but I'm glad that he didn't interfere with what I had going on. Everyone that I asked to come was already here except for Ariel. I was only gonna wait for her for about another two minutes before I went in the church. The parking lot was packed to capacity, and I was glad about it. Ariel's car pulled up, so we all got out of our cars. I greeted everyone and thanked them for coming with me. I was surprised to see my mother, Ms. Candace, and her husband there, but I was glad everyone showed up.

When we got in the church, everyone was just getting seated. The usher gave us a row to ourselves, and I made sure that I was sitting on the end so I could get up when the time is right. The service had started, and I must admit that I was really enjoying the songs that were being sung. For a minute I thought about not going through with my plans, but hell with that. I've been waiting for damn near ten years to get some closure, and today was my day. The singing had now come to a stop, and people started being called to give presentations and speeches, so I knew it wouldn't be much longer before my name was called. I called the church a couple of weeks ago and asked to be put on the program because I had a special presentation that I wanted to give to Pastor Wilson and his wife.

"Before we end this part of the service, we have a young lady by the name of Nyla Price, that has a special presentation that she would like to give our pastor."

Zaire and the rest of the family all looked up at me in confusion. I got up and walked to the front of the church with my purse. I thought I would be more nervous than I was, but I was actually good. The lady that called me up passed me the mic. I closed my eyes before I began to speak. I could see people with their cells out as if they were recording, but I didn't care.

"Good morning, church."

"Good morning," the church said back in unison.

"I'm here today to present some really special things to Pastor Wilson." I turned to face Bishop and his wife before I started to speak.

"The reason that I'm here is because Pastor Wilson and I have a little history. About eight years ago, I met Pastor Wilson, better known to me as Bishop, in the Poconos at a party. He asked to buy me a drink but I declined, so he decided to spike the drink I was already drinking. I didn't know at the time that he dropped something in my drink, until I started feeling funny and needed air. When I walked out the building, I was followed by him and a group of guys. I was in and out of consciousness, but I could hear everything. Your pastor instructed a man to rape me, but he told him no. however, your pastor wasn't very happy with that answer, so he pulled a gun on the guy and forced him to do it. I laid there on the ground, pleading for my life and the guy that he forced leaned in my ear and told me he didn't want to rape me, but he had to, or he would die.

I told him I was a virgin and pleaded some more, but he had to do what he had to do to save his own life like anyone else would. The guy that raped me promised to be gentle, and he kept his promise, but Bishop wasn't having that. So he made the first guy get off me and brutally raped me. He hit me in my face as I begged him to stop. He was rough and he could care less that he was hurting me. I would have given my life to have the first guy to do it than this sick bastard," I stated as the tears fell from my face. I could hear the church going crazy and all kinds of shocked noises coming from the church. Bishop started yelling that I was lying, and his wife just stared at him. I could tell she was confused and didn't know if she believed me or not.

"Get her out of here! She's standing in this church spreading lies and making false accusations! I don't know this woman! She must have me confused with someone else!" Bishop yelled. But I kept talking and I dared anyone to try to take this mic before I was finished talking. I saw Zaire get up from his seat and started walking towards me. I prayed he wasn't coming to interfere because not even he would be able to stop me. But instead of stopping me, he grabbed my hand, stood by my side and encouraged me to continue.

"How dare you stand here in this church and call yourself a man of God when you can't even be honest with them about your past? How can you ask them to follow a man that's not even man nor Christian enough to admit your truth? Church, I know this comes as a surprise, but this man did rape me along with others. He stole my innocence. I had to go to counseling, and I had nightmares about my attack for years. I can prove that he did rape me and that he does know me," I stated, and Zaire looked at me with wide eyes as curiosity took over his stare. I reached into my purse and pulled out the clothes that I was wearing the night of the rape. The church started going crazy. I closed my eyes and let the tears fall freely.

"My husband did no such thing," his wife finally spoke up. Before I could respond, Zaire took the mic out of my hand and started to talk.

"Ma'am, with all due respect, my wife has no reason to lie. I know for a fact that he raped her and the reason I know is because I was there. I am the man he threatened to kill if I didn't do it. I had to do years of therapy and haven't seen Bishop since that night. Crazily, I met Nyla at the movie theater with no clue that she was the woman I was forced to rape. Ironically, we hit it off and ended up getting married, but it wasn't until my honeymoon that I put it together that she was the woman. So, Bishop, what you not gonna do is lie to this woman about something we know is the truth. You already ruined her life, don't paint her out to be a liar," Zaire told him before giving me the mic. I was just about done here, but I needed to get a few more things off my chest. Then I would be done with this forever. I walked up close and personal to Bishop and stared him in his eyes.

"Look me in my eyes in front of your entire congregation and tell me that you didn't rape me. And if you say that you didn't, I will call the cops here. I will tell them what you did and have them take my clothes to test them. I guarantee you they will find your DNA on my clothes!" I yelled angrily. "Tell your church that you're a rapist!" I yelled once more. Shockingly, Bishop dropped to his knees and started asking God for forgiveness. Then he looked at me with tears in his eyes.

"I'm sorry. I was young and dumb, please forgive me!" he pleaded, and I just stood there crying. It felt like I was nailed to the floor.

"I hated you and wished death upon you on many days, but now I realize that you're just scum, and you're not worth it. I should have never given you that much power over me, so yes, I forgive you but not for you but for me. I thought about sending you to jail, but you're not even worth that," I told him. I looked up to God as if I was looking in his eyes.

"Forgive me, Lord for not forgiving him sooner for my own good," I said to God, and I swear it felt like the weight of my shoulder was lifted off me. Now I could move my feet. I really needed this. Just as I was about to walk away, Zaire punched the shit out of the Bishop.

"That was for my wife and this is for me," Zaire yelled before punching him again. With that, I dropped the mic and headed towards the door, still in tears as my family met me in the middle of the aisle. We hugged tightly before walking out the church.

Chapter Eighteen

Tasha

I was sitting at the church crying my eyes out as I watched my best friend confront and expose her rapist. I don't think there was a dry eye in the building. Nyla spoke her truth with so much pain laced in her voice. I hated to see her in so much pain, but I was glad that she finally got to let it out. I just prayed that she got the closure that she needed. We all walked out of the church and hugged and cried some more. After getting ourselves together, we were all headed over to Nyla's for Sunday dinner. I heard someone call my name and I wasn't sure who it was. I turned around to see who it was and I thought I was looking at a ghost. I was looking in the face of the woman that gave birth to me. I just froze. It's been years since I've seen my mom or heard anything about her for that matter. If I could be honest, I just knew she was dead somewhere.

"Oh my God, Tasha, you're so beautiful," she stated as she stood there with tears in her eyes.

"I thought you were dead." I could feel the blood in my body warming up as my emotions seemed like they were about to erupt. Nyla walked over asking was I okay, and for some reason, that question brought a wave of tears.

"I can't believe that you two are still friends. You're beautiful, Nyla," my mom stated.

"Thank you, Miss Pamela," Nyla replied.

"Of course, we're still friends; we're more than friends. She's the only family that I have, thanks to you."

"Tasha, I'm sorry. I should have been a better mother, but I didn't know how to be a mom and a junkie," she cried. "I thought about you every day, but I was glad when you went to stay with Nyla and her family. I never came to get you because I knew you would be better off with them."

"Nyla, we're gonna head over to the house and get things started," Ms. Candace said to Nyla.

"Charles?" My mom called out, causing me and Nyla to look at one another.

"Pamela?" The creepy guy that gave me bad vibes, replied. It was something about that man that made me freak out every time I had to be around him. I tried to avoid him at all cost, but that wasn't possible. He's never done anything to me or said anything out the way to me. It was just something about him.

"Wait, y'all know each other?" My mom asked oddly with her face scrunched up.

"Pamela, I haven't seen you in years," Charles answered.

"Well, how would I see you? I haven't seen you since the day you walked out on me and left me to raise a child alone," my mom shot back. My chest tightened up, and shit was becoming too much for me to deal with. It almost sounded like she was indicating that I was his daughter unless she had another child that I wasn't aware of.

"Pamela, this is not the time to do this," Charles replied.

"Mom, what's going on?"

"Tasha, this is your dad," my mom said, and I swear as soon as the words left her mouth, it felt like the whole world stopped.

"Pamela, what the fuck are you talking about?" Charles yelled.

"This is Tasha, your daughter, the one you left sitting in the living room crying over you at the age of three," my mom shot back. Today was too much, and I needed to get away. I needed to breathe because it felt like my breath was caught in my throat. At this point, all I could do was cry.

"I can't do this," I stated, running away from everyone. I could hear everyone calling after me, but I just kept running. I couldn't believe the way this day turned out. Everything was full of drama, lies, and secrets. I couldn't believe that I ran into my mom, who I haven't seen in years just for her to reveal that my boyfriend's stepfather was my biological father. This was too much for anyone to handle. I never wanted to see either of them again. I heard a horn beeping, followed by Cameron's voice. Cameron pulled up on the side of me and demanded for me to get in the car. I didn't argue with him, I just did as he said.

When I got in the car, all I could do was cry, Cameron didn't pressure me to talk, he just drove in silence and let me be. We got to his house in no time. When we pulled up, he walked around and opened my door. When we got in the house, Cameron pulled me close and hugged me tightly as I sobbed on his shoulders. I cried for what seemed like forever before I got myself together. I replayed the entire event from today, and it was a hot ass mess. I found out that my mom was alive and that my boyfriend's stepfather was my dad. I thought about my mom saying I was crying for him. Which means at some point he was in my life then abandoned me just like my mom. I never wanted to see or hear from either of them as long as I lived.

"Baby, I know today was a lot, but do you want to talk about what the fuck just happened?"

"Honestly, I don't know what to say to be honest. It was already an emotional time watching my best friend confront her attacker. Then I ran into my mom, who I thought was dead, just to learn that your stepdad is my dad. This shit is just sick and twisted, and my heart is heavy right now. I want to be there for Nyla today, but I just can't. I just need some time," I said to Cameron.

"I understand. Do you want me to leave for a few hours or do you want me to stay here with you?" I hoped like hell I didn't hurt his feelings, but I really felt like I needed just a little time to myself.

"Honestly, I just need some time alone for a couple of hours. If I feel like coming out or if I need you, I'll call you. Cameron, I really do love and appreciate you," I told him.

"I love you too, Tasha. Call me if you need anything. I'm about to pick up the baby and check on my mom then head over to Zaire and Nyla's house," he said before leaving.

Cameron was only gone for about twenty minutes before I regretted asking him to leave. I laid there on the couch as all kinds of thoughts took over my brain. I wondered if he always knew who I was but just never said anything. I thought about how good my mom looked, and I wondered how long she's been off of drugs, or if I had other siblings? I heard her say that she thought about me every day but what she didn't say was she was looking for me. I was driving myself crazy with all my loose thoughts that I ended up crying myself to sleep.

******

A few hours later, I woke up and Cameron still wasn't home, I didn't even realize that I had slept for so long. When I sat up, my head was pounding so bad, I got up and took some Motrin. I grabbed my phone, and I had so many missed calls and text messages from Cameron and Nyla and a few numbers that I didn't know. I dialed Cameron's number, but he didn't answer. I was about to call Nyla, but before I got to dial her number, I heard the door open, and it was Cameron and Serenity. He passed her to me so he could go back out to the car. As soon as I held my daughter and looked into her eyes, I felt a sense of calmness come over me. Cameron walked back in with what looked like food, and I was glad because a bitch was starving.

"Let me get her ready for bed; you need to eat and take a shower. The day has been hella crazy," Cameron said, taking Serenity from my arms. I got up to use the bathroom then warmed up a plate and stuffed my face. I wanted this day to be over with. After eating, I took a long hot shower, and let my thoughts run free. I had some many thoughts about life, my parents, and why wasn't I worth change. Ever since I was a little girl, I vowed to be the best mother I could be, and I meant every word.

After my shower, I went and laid down in the bed. Cameron climbed in the bed and wrapped his arms around my waist. He held me all night as we slept. I regret sneaking around with Brandon on Cameron. Cameron could be rude and arrogant sometimes, but he was a great guy and an even greater father.

*****

It's been two weeks since that drama happened with my mom and supposed to be dad. I've been keeping myself busy in my shop that I opened last week, thanks to Cameron and Nyla. Nyla did all the decorating and my shop was bomb. I've been so busy that I barely had time to think about the craziness. Nyla and Cameron think that I owe it to myself to at least have a conversation with my mom. I've thought about it, but I wouldn't even know how to reach her, I knew at some point we would talk, but I just didn't feel like I was ready at this moment. Everything was so fresh, and I had so much anger built up in me, and I knew the conversation would turn into something bigger.

My receptionist told me, I had two clients coming in today, one previous client and a new client. I finished putting the final touches to my makeup station. I loved doing hair and makeup. I was happy that I was now working for myself instead of working for someone else. My first client came in for her makeup appointment, and that took about a half hour. Once I was finished up with her makeup, I took my lunch break because I was starving. I walked down to the Chinese store to get some wings and fries. When I got back to the shop, I went into my office and fucked those wings and fries up. For some reason, that shit was extra good.

It was now time for my hair appointment, and on que, my receptionist knocked on my door to tell me that my client was here. When I walked out, I couldn't believe that the client was my mom. My entire demeanor changed. I couldn't believe that she showed up at my workplace; this wasn't the time or the place.

"Tasha, I'm sorry for coming to your workplace, but I knew the only way you would talk to me was for me to make an appointment. I don't really want the services, but I am willing to pay for them just to get your time," she stated.

"I'm not happy about being forced to do something that I'm not ready to do. I really hope you can say all you need to say in ten minutes," I told her.

"I'll take all that I can get," my mom responded. We walked towards my office so we could have some privacy. My mom didn't waste any time talking.

"Tasha, I know I wasn't a mother to you, and I'm sorry for that. I let my drug habit get the best of me and take over my life. Once I lost my job, everything went downhill from there. I was willing to do anything to get it, and that included sleeping around with different men. Me and Charles were together for about four years, and it was the happiest time of my life. But as soon as I had you, he started to change, staying out all night. When I would confront him, he would beat the shit out of me.

That lasted for about two years, then finally he decided he didn't want to be with me anymore. So, he packed up and, on his way out, you screamed and hollered for him. Charles yelled at you for the first time and it broke your heart. You let out a cry that I've never heard before. That day broke my heart, watching you cry over a man that didn't want you. When I saw him at the church that day was the first time I saw him since the day he walked out.

I started getting high to take the pain away, but all it did was fuck my life up and cause me to neglect you in the process. I know you felt like I abandoned you, but the truth was I knew Nyla's parents could give you a better life, and you turned out great. I hope that you will forgive me, Tasha. I love you so much. Sometimes as parents, you have to do what's best for the child even if that means you're not the one to give them the best," my mom cried. Tears fell down my face listening to her talk.

"Why wasn't I worth you changing, mom? Did you ever come look for me or did you just say hell with me?" I asked.

"It doesn't work like that, Tasha. I wanted to stop, but I was addicted to drugs. If I could just stop, I would have if it was that easy. After you left, things just went downhill for me. I lost everything. I lost you, my job, my house, and my self-respect. It's easy for outsiders to say you could have stopped. Do you think I wanted to get up and suck dick everyday for a hit? Do you think living on the streets was something that I wanted to do? It took me to hit rock bottom and almost die to get my shit together. I was gang-raped and beat so bad that I was unrecognizable. I was in the hospital for two damn months. Most of the time I was there, I was in a medically induced coma. I had no family to visit me, no way to find you. If it wasn't for the nurse that was caring for me, I don't know where I would be today. I've been clean for two years now. After nurse Shelia nursed me back to health, she became a friend and invited me to church.

I decided to take her up on her offer because I had tried everything but God, so I knew it couldn't hurt. God has really been blessing me, and my biggest blessing thus far was running into you," my mom told me. After hearing her story, I felt bad. I wished that things didn't have to get so bad for her to get right.

"I'm sorry you had to go through that, but I'm glad that you got the help you needed. Do I have any other siblings?"

"No, that's the one thing that I vowed, which was to never have another child. I'm sorry that I failed you as a mother," my mom apologized. She sounded sincere. I wasn't sure if I could ever forgive, but I think I owed it to myself to at least give her a chance. She's been through enough already, so there was no need for me to punish her even more.

"You grew up to be beautiful, Tasha. You have your own shop. You did well for yourself. I'm proud of you. I'm not going to take up any more of your time, just know that I love you and I always will."

"I have a daughter; she's almost six months, and her name is Serenity. I don't know where to go from here, and I'm not sure if I would ever be able to forgive you because everything is fresh," I told my mom honestly.

"I'm gonna say this, then I'm gonna get out of your hair. You need to forgive me but not for me, but for yourself. It's the only way you will ever be able to move forward and stop being so angry and resentful. I can't tell you when to forgive, but the longer you wait, the longer it will take you to move forward," my mom stated.

I took in what she was saying, and I knew that she was right, but today wasn't gonna be the day. I needed to think and process this. I never thought that I'd see my mom again and hearing that she was raped and beat so bad that she was in a coma was a hard pill to swallow. I never stopped loving my mom, but I haven't had one of those in a very long time.

"I can't make any promises, but I will try. I'm just not ready right at this very moment," I replied honestly.

"Fair enough, I understand, but here take my number. If you change your mind or whenever you're ready to talk. I would love to get to know and meet my granddaughter. I fucked up with you, but I would like to get it right with her. I bet she's beautiful just like you." My mom passed me a piece of paper and I put it on my desk. I was ready for this family reunion to be over; it was too overwhelming.

Before my mom walked out of my office she turned and faced me. "Tasha, I really do love you no matter what it seems like, and I'll spend the rest of my life trying to show you if you let me."

I didn't say anything, I just let her walk out the door. I sat at my desk trying to gather my thoughts. I decided since I didn't have any more clients that I would call it a day. I swear after the last few weeks that I had I needed a girl's night out with my best friend. I needed to have a couple of drinks and shake my ass.

Chapter Nineteen

Candace

I was sitting at chemotherapy thinking about my life and how much of it I wasted on getting high. Now that I was ready to live and was the happiest that I've ever been, I was now fighting for my life. Cancer wasn't no joke, and it was taking people out of here like night and day. I wanted to see my grandkids grow up, but I wasn't sure if that would happen. The only thing I was sure about was that I was going to try to live. I would fight everyday that God let me wake up. I had the greatest sons any mother could ask for. They made sure that I was well taken care of. Even when I was getting high, they would still come and check on me. Zaire more so than Cameron. He was always so angry and bitter.

Cameron always had a bad temper. One minute he could be laughing and joking with you, and next, he could be punching you in the face. Zaire was the calm before the storm. He was calm and cool, but once he reached his breaking point, he could be worse than Cameron. Cameron and Zaire paid for me to get treatment at the Cancer center that they always advertised on tv. This was my second week, and so far, things seemed to be going pretty well. Charles and I haven't really been seeing eye to eye since the day we ran into his supposed to be baby mom at the church. Learning that he had a daughter that he failed to mention had me bothered. Then to find out that his daughter was pretty much my daughter in-law.

I tried reaching out to Tasha a few times, but she wasn't ready to talk about it, and I didn't blame her. Cameron said she wasn't dealing with it too well. I was pissed at Charles, because he acted as if he didn't care that Tasha was his daughter and that bothered me, causing us to argue all the time. I know that I won't get the mother of the year award, but I've always loved and cherished my kids. I wanted to be in their life and take care of them, but my addiction had me fucked up. When I was finished with chemo, I went home and got in bed to get some rest. I had to do chemo once a week, and the boys took turns taking me. Someone knocking on the front door caused me to wake up. I opened the door, and I was surprised to see Tasha and my granddaughter. I was actually glad she came by, plus I missed my grandbaby.

"Hey, Ms. Candace. How are you?"

"Hey, baby. I'm good; I was just getting some rest. I had chemo today, and how many times do I have to tell you to call me mom or mom Candace?"

"Oh, I'm sorry. I didn't mean to interrupt your sleep," Tasha apologized.

"It's fine I need to start dinner anyway. So what brings you by and let me see my baby, " I told her, taking the baby from her arms.

"I really just needed someone to talk to. I needed to talk to someone who had a drug addiction," she stated, putting her head down. I guess she felt uncomfortable mentioning that I had a drug problem.

"Tasha, you don't have to be embarrassed to say I had a drug problem because I'm not embarrassed. But what's going on, baby?"

"It's my mom, I'm not sure if you're aware but two weeks ago was the first time I've seen my mom since I was a teenager. Well, she came to see me yesterday, and for some reason, I don't know how to forgive her. She explained that she was on drugs and didn't want to abandon me, but she was sick, and the drugs kept her from doing what she knew was the right thing to do. A part of me wants to forgive her, and a part of me don't know how. I mean, she looks good and sounds sincere. I just don't know what to do."

"Tasha, I love you like my own, so I'm gonna keep it real with you, and I'm going to be speaking out of experience. You can't hold your mom accountable for anything that she did while being on drugs. That shit takes over your life. You want to do right, but you can't. It's like a baby that watches everyone around them walk. They wanna walk, but their feet won't move. Tasha, you already lost time with her, don't continue to punish her for something she's trying to overcome or have overcome already. The last thing you want her to do is feel like she's still not good enough and get back out there. Usually, it takes a tragedy and for you to hit rock bottom to get clean," I told Tasha honestly.

"What made you stop?" she asked.

"Honestly, it was Zaire. One day him and Cameron came by and caught a guy roughing me up because I owed him money for drugs. Cameron and my nephew roughed him up, but I begged them to stop and not to hurt him because he had the best drugs around. Cameron and Brian looked at me like a disgrace, but Zaire took the boy outside and paid my debt. I noticed when I would go get drugs, the guy wouldn't charge me. I knew Zaire was the reason why I didn't have to pay, and it made me feel like shit. Because I knew he was so worried about me getting hurt, he would rather pay for it then to see me tricking or get killed over drugs. I still did it for a little longer, but I gradually stopped. I had put my boys through enough, and they deserved to have a mother at some point in their lives. The day I was bold enough to ask my sons not to harm a man because he had good drugs was the day I knew I had hit my rock bottom.

I can't tell you what to do, but you need to let the past be just that. If she's in church and has been clean for more than six months, my guess would be that she's truly done with that shit and trying to move on. So my suggestion would be for you to put the past behind you and spend as much time as you can with her before you no longer have an option because she's dying," I told her with tear-filled eyes. Having this conversation with Tasha caused me to get emotional.

"I'm so sorry. I guess that was a bit insensitive. I didn't mean to make you cry," Tasha apologized.

"I'm not crying because you said anything wrong. I'm crying because I didn't spend enough time with my own sons, and now that I finally got my shit together and started having a great relationship with them, that may be cut short all because I have cancer. I want to see my grandkids grow up. I just need you to promise me something. Promise me that when I do pass away that you will take good care of my son. Cameron loves you, and I know that in the near future, you'll be his wife. Just please don't hurt my son, and he's gonna need you to be there for him whenever the day comes. Cameron plays the tough role, but he will break when the time comes for me to leave this earth," I cried. I didn't realize how much this was bothering me. I guess I needed this talk just as much as Tasha did. Tasha got up from her seat and hugged me tightly as I cried on her shoulders.

"I swear I'll take care of him, mom, but I know God has more for you. He wouldn't bring you this far to leave you," Tasha stated. I hoped she was right because the thought of dying was scary.

"Tasha, you and Nyla are the daughters I always wanted. I'm so glad that both of my sons found great women to hold them down. I've never said this to you before, but I love you," I told Tasha sincerely. Tasha was about to speak until the door opened. I knew that it wasn't nobody but Charles, and I also knew things were about to get awkward.

"I love you too, mom. I think I should get going, and just so you know I think you're pretty dope," she said with a smile before getting up to leave.

"Candace, you could have told me we had company." Charles started his shit as soon as he walked in the door.

"First off, Charles, don't come in this house with that shit, and she's not company. She's our daughter, and you need to step up and act like it," I snapped. I was sick of his shit. Charles has been acting crazy since he found out that Tasha was his daughter, and I was about sick of it. I had enough to deal with. The room fell silent, and everything was awkward just like I thought it would be.

"It's okay, mom. He didn't want me then, and he still don't want me now, but it's his loss and not mine. I grew up to be a great woman without the help of him or my momma, and although I'm upset with her too at least, she's trying to make things right. Take care and I'll be by to see you soon," Tasha stated before walking out. As soon as Tasha left, I let Charles' selfish ass have it. We went back and forth for what seemed like an hour. I didn't even bother to cook dinner. I made my ass a sandwich, took a shower, and went to sleep and left Charles up looking stupid.

Chapter Twenty

Ariel

"Jasmine, I can't do this shit anymore. Nyla will never forgive me if I stay in this relationship with you. I love you I swear I do, but this is just a disaster waiting to happen," I told my girlfriend.

"So, let me get this straight, you're breaking up with me over something that I have no control over? How can you love me, and yet you can just toss me to the side like I never meant anything?" Jasmine shot back

"Jasmine, why the fuck can't you see how crazy this is and how much drama this will cause with me and my family when they found out who you are?" I yelled. Jasmine was starting to piss me off.

"Ariel, I understand that it may cause a little friction and be uncomfortable at first, but that shit don't have shit to do with us."

"So, you think that when I walk up to my sister and tell her that I am in a relationship with the sister of the nigga that brutally raped her, all she's going to be is uncomfortable?" I yelled with tears in my eyes.

"My sister is just now getting closure after all of these years, and you want me to tell her that? You sound stupid, Jasmine. I love you, but I'm done. This it's just too much," I told her.

"You know what, Ariel? Fuck you and your fucking sister? You can't be with me because I'm related to the man that raped your sister? But your sister can marry the man that also raped her? Man, both of y'all bitches is crazy!" Jasmine screamed loudly. For some reason, something took over my body, and I rushed her, and we started fighting. I couldn't believe that she had said some shit like that. Jasmine pushed me down so hard that I fell on the floor, and before I could get up, she darted out the door. I just sat on the floor crying. This shit was too much. It seemed like we could never catch a break in this family, and the crazy thing was most of our drama and issues had something to do with Nyla. I hated to feel like this, but I was starting to resent my own sister for shit that wasn't even her fault.

I found out that Jasmine was Bishop's sister the day that Nyla confronted him at his church. And since that day, our relationship has been in shambles. We argued everyday over this shit. I didn't think it was a great idea to stay in the relationship, but she feels like she didn't do shit, and she was just as disgusted that her brother did that shit. Jasmine and her brother also fought over this. She stopped speaking to him and everything, and that was over a month ago. Nyla was doing so good and finally put it behind her. How was I supposed to be the one that makes her relive it? Every day that I'm with Jasmine, she would be reminded of her attack, and that wasn't fair. And I didn't want that to be on my conscious.

Life hasn't been the easiest for either of us, but we make the best out of the cards that has been dealt to us. Losing our parents at a young age was hard, and being raised by your brother who's only a couple of years older than you was a little rough. Brandon did what he could to raise us and make sure we did something meaningful with our lives while trying to do something with his life as well. But shit still wasn't easy. We needed a mother in our life. Hell, we didn't even have a mother figure to help guide us. Nyla's attack was the first real drama. Brandon felt guilty like he was partly responsible for allowing her to go. Brandon wasn't having it at first, but the help of persuasion from me, he decided to let her go. Nyla begged for me to come with her, but I didn't want to go because I was planning to spend the weekend with my boyfriend. I wasn't beat to be stuck around a bunch of teenage high school graduates. I had just turned twenty, so I wasn't beat. I honestly blamed Tasha for leaving Nyla by herself at a party that she begged Nyla to go too. At times I thought she was involved somehow, but I let that theory go as time went on.

Hours had passed since me and Jasmine's argument, and I was missing her like crazy. I wanted to talk to Brandon about it. Him and I just started talking again a couple of weeks ago. The truth was I was still feeling some type of way about how he spoke to me when we got into it. Me and my siblings never really fought because we were all close-knit. They might upset me, but I loved those two more than life itself. Outside of our relationships, each other was all we had. A knock at that door brought me from my thoughts. I went to the door and it was Nyla and Tasha.

"Damn bitch, why you didn't answer your phone? I have to pee so damn bad," Nyla said, brushing past me to get to the bathroom.

"My bad, I was in the middle of something with Jasmine," I replied.

"Girl, this bitch was about to be on the side of the road, she had to pee so bad. The crazy thing was she just used the bathroom before we left the mall," Tasha chimed in.

"Where is Jasmine?" Nyla asked instantly, changing my mood.

"We broke up, and no, I don't want to talk about it right now," I said in one breath.

"Oh my God, I'm sorry to hear that. What the hell happened? Y'all was just fine," Nyla pried. I let my emotions get the best of me, and I started crying uncontrollably. I contemplated if I should be honest or just lie. I decided to just be honest and tell her because I was sick of the secrets and drama. I took a deep breath before speaking.

"Nyla, I don't know how to tell you this, but the reason why me and Jasmine broke up was because of you-" I told her, and she cut me off.

"Because of me? What the hell did I do?" she asked confusingly.

"You didn't do anything, but it's a very small world. I found out that Jasmine's brother is the guy that attacked you," I told her. The room fell silent, and Tasha's mouth was hanging open so damn wide that I could see her tonsils. Nyla laughed hysterically, and me and Tasha just looked at her like she was fucking crazy. I didn't find shit funny unless she was trying to laugh to keep from crying.

"Best friend, are you good? Because you're laughing but ain't shit funny," Tasha said to Nyla, taking the words right out of my mouth.

"I'm laughing because I just think it's funny. How ironic is that my sister is in a relationship with my rapist sister?" Nyla replied and shook her head.

"Nyla, I know that's why I broke it off. It's just too much; this family can't seem to escape the drama. When she found out, she was disgusted. Her and her brother haven't spoken since she found out what he did. But her and I have been arguing everyday about it. I told her I couldn't do that to you."

"Ariel, I really appreciate you having my back, but you don't have to break up with Jasmine because she happens to be related to that sick pervert. Once I got the closure that I needed, I've been better than ever. And I'm not worried about him. He can't hurt me anymore. I exposed him for who he really was and made him admit to his entire congregation what he did to me. Although I'm sure he only apologized because I had him by the balls, he still did it. Are you in love with Jasmine?" Nyla asked.

I was shocked and lost for words at Nyla's reaction to what I told her. I guess my baby sister truly got the closure that she was looking for.

"Yeah, I'm in love with her. This is the best relationship I've been in," I told her honestly.

"Well, who am I to stand in between your happiness? Hell, I married my rapist. When I found out, I loved him so much that I stayed with him and I've never been happier. So, I say go get your woman but just know I'll never be in the same room with that prick," Nyla stated. I was so happy that she gave me her blessing because, even though I broke it off with Jasmine, I knew I would have been miserable without her. Jasmine made me happy, and her sex game was amazing, so that would have been a major loss on my part.

"I love you so much, Nyla, and thanks for your blessing," I said, hugging her tightly.

"It's nothing to thank me for, and I love you too, Ariel. Now let me get out of here before my husband have a fit that I'm not back yet," Nyla said while walking towards the door.

After they left, I picked up the phone to call Jasmine, but it went straight to voicemail, so I left her message telling her to call me. Jasmine must have still been pissed because I called at least a dozen times, and she didn't answer the phone or my texts. I was starting to get worried because I thought she would have responded by now. I decided to cook dinner, take a shower, and put on something sexy to wait for her to return home or at least call.

Hours later, I still hadn't heard from Jasmine. My feelings was hurt as I came to realize that we were really over. I ended up crying myself to sleep. The next morning when I woke up, I hoped that I was dreaming, and that Jasmine was in the kitchen making breakfast. Except when I walked in the kitchen there was no sign of her. I flopped down on the couch and looked at my phone to see if I somehow missed any calls or text from her, but there was nothing. I did have a text from Brandon and Nyla checking up on me. I tried calling

Jasmine's phone once more, but still nothing. She must have had me blocked.

I loved Jasmine, but fuck her. I wasn't about to sit around and pout over her all day. I knew that things got a little heated yesterday, but that was no reason to ignore all my calls or text. I decided to get dressed and grab some breakfast by myself to clear my mind. Once I was dressed, I got in my car and drove to IHOP. I walked in and was about to be seated when I heard Jasmine's voice. I looked over and she was sitting there with some girl and I instantly became enraged. I walked over to the table and stood there for a second before she realized that I was standing there. Jasmine looked shocked to see me.

"So, we get into an argument, and this is what the fuck you do? Stay out all night and then get up and come to breakfast with some bitch? Who the fuck is this, Jasmine?" I yelled. I knew I was probably making a fool out of myself, but I was too mad to care.

"Ariel, you need to calm your little ass down," Jasmine stated calmly.

"Okay, you don't want to answer me? I'll find out one way or another. Who the fuck are you?" I asked the bitch that Jasmine was sitting with.

"I'm sorry you have the wrong idea. I'm Jasmine's cousin, Leah. You must be Ariel," The girl stated with a smirk and put her hand out for a handshake. I just looked at her hand and rolled my eyes.

"Jasmine, fucking answer me!" I yelled loudly. Jasmine jumped up from the table, grabbed my arm and damn near dragged me out the restaurant.

"What the fuck is your problem, Ariel? First, you break up with me, then you put your hands on me, and now you're here at the restaurant showing your ass and being rude to my cousin? How the fuck did you even know I was here? What the fuck is going on with you?" Jasmine snapped.

"First off, I didn't know you were here; I was coming to get some breakfast. Secondly, I called you all night long, and you didn't even have enough respect to respond. Then I walk in on you eating breakfast with some chick, and you don't know what's wrong with me?"

"I didn't answer your call because I turned my phone off. I needed some time, and I thought we were broken up, so I'm not obligated to respond to your calls or explain who I'm having breakfast with. I'm not going to go through this back and forth shit with you. I'm not with all this drama shit. You either want to be with me or you don't. So, what the fuck is it, Ariel? Are we together or not?" I took a deep breath and calmed my little ass down. I couldn't afford to fuck this up. Jasmine was right; she wasn't with the crazy shit. Normally I wasn't either, but I was tripping.

"Look, Jasmine, I'm sorry about yesterday and today. I was wrong about us. I was miserable without you, and we haven't even been apart for twenty-four hours yet. So, to answer your question, we're together," I said. Jasmine just stared at me for a moment before grabbing my face and kissing me passionately. I was so glad that we were back on good terms.

"Now let's go, your rude ass owes my cousin an apology with your crazy ass," Jasmine said smacking my ass. When we walked, I walked over to the table, and Jasmine's cousin looked up from her phone.

"I apologize for my behavior; I shouldn't have acted that way. Please forgive me. I'm Ariel," I said, holding my hand out. She just looked at my hand then laughed.

"I'm just kidding. It's nice to meet you, Ariel. You two are sick and definitely in love. I'm going to go and let you ladies talk. Jasmine, I'll talk to you later and it was nice meeting you, Ariel," Leah said before leaving.

"Nice meeting you too." I ordered my food and something to drink, and me and Jasmine talked and apologized to one another.

"Hurry up on that food. I'm about to eat the shit out that pussy, you gonna learn today not to pull no shit like that ever again," Jasmine stated. I knew she wasn't playing either and I was looking forward to it.

"I can't wait," I told her with a sexy smile. I never ate so fast in my life because I couldn't wait to get home to get some of Jasmine's loving.

Chapter Twenty-One

Nyla

"Babe, dinner is ready," I yelled upstairs to Zaire. I just finished making dinner, and then I planned to have a romantic evening with my husband. I made ribs, steak, mashed potatoes, and corn.

"Damn baby, this looks good as hell," Zaire said, smacking my ass. "Damn, that ass getting fatter."

I just blushed and walked to my seat. I had candles lit and music playing, it was about to go down tonight. After dinner, I went to take a shower and slip on something comfortable while Zaire did the dishes. I walked into the bathroom and hopped in the shower. I guess my husband couldn't wait for me to get out the shower because he decided to join me. I was washing up when he got in.

"Let me help you with that," he said, taking the rag to wash my precious jewel. I let out a soft moan as he rubbed my clitoris in a circular motion. Zaire washed the suds off my body, then picked me up, carried me to the bedroom, and laid me on the bed. Zaire didn't waste any time getting to business. Zaire kissed my moist warm folds in between my thighs and my center pulsated and tingled with pleasure. After creaming in my husband's mouth, Zaire got up. Zaire slowly entered his stiffness into my wetness and slow stroked me while rubbing my swollen pearl in a circular motion.

"Ahh, baby, this feels so good," I moaned in Zaire's ear. My center clamped around his erection and my juices ran freely. Zaire's strokes sped up. He palmed my ass as he released his seeds into my vagina.

"Shit, Nyla! I'm cumming!" Zaire groaned loudly before collapsing on the bed. After catching our breath, I started off round two. After hours of me and my husband exploring each other's body, we finally drifted off to sleep.

The next morning, I got up not feeling too well. I sat up on the edge of the bed but had to run to the bathroom. I barely made it to the toilet before puke was flying out of my mouth. I swear it seemed like I was throwing up forever. I guess the sound woke Zaire up from his sleep.

"Baby, you good?" Zaire asked, walking into the bathroom. I wiped my mouth before answering.

"I guess something I ate last night didn't agree with me," I told him. I thought I was finally done, so I got up and brushed my teeth and washed my face.

"I feel fine, that food was everything last night," Zaire replied. Zaire walked out of the bathroom, and once I was finished, I sat back on the edge of the bed because I was still feeling a little nauseous. He walked backed in the room with a can of ginger ale. I knew that would get me right. Zaire opened the can and passed it to me. I took a few sips, and after the second swig, I had to run back to the bathroom. I was back hanging over the toilet, throwing up my insides.

"Let me get you some crackers and see if that works, " Zaire said. He came back with the crackers. I ate a few, and they seemed to settle my stomach a little.

A few hours later, I was feeling better. I was hungry as shit, but I was scared to eat. I knew I had to get better because tonight was Zaire's grand opening of his lounge, so I had to be on point. I decided to eat something light, and surprisingly, I kept it down. I got my clothes out that I was wearing tonight. Zaire had to run out and run a few errands, so I decided to take an hour nap. I laid down and fell right to sleep.

*****

"Nyla, get up. Why aren't you dressed yet? We gonna be late", Zaire said, waking me up from my sleep.

"Oh my God, I didn't realize that I was sleep for so long. I swear it's not going to take me long to get dressed." I hopped up and took a quick shower. I lotioned my body down and put my clothes on. I wore a navy-blue romper with a pair of silver stilettos and silver accessories. I wore my hair in a high ponytail and threw on some light makeup. I looked in the mirror and I was satisfied with my look. Zaire walked in the room and I damn near came on myself. He looked so fucking good. He was rocking a pair of white jeans with a white shirt and a customized navy-blue blazer.

"Damn baby, you rocking the hell out of that romper. If we weren't already running late, you would have got fucked before making it out this door," Zaire said, kissing me on my neck.

"Thanks, babe. You looking good your damn self and if you keep kissing my neck like that, we gonna be running even later," I flirted because I was serious, I was already horny as hell.

"Well, we better get going, but I'm gonna fuck the shit out of you when we get back home. Ain't gone be no lovemaking tonight, so I hope you're ready," Zaire warned.

A couple hours later, the lounge was packed to capacity, and the DJ had this place lit. Of course, we were all in the VIP section. Tasha and I danced with one another while Zaire did some mingling. When my husband made it back to the VIP, I was feeling it, and I decided to give my husband a lap dance. That was just a sample of what he was going to get when we got home. Brandon walked up looking good; he was with his best friend Joey and two girls. The way the one girl was hanging onto my brother's arm, you could tell they were fucking. And if they wasn't, they would be soon. I walked up and hugged my brother. Joey was eye-fucking me, and I don't even think he even realized it. But Zaire did and let it be known.

"Damn Joey, I know my wife is fine and all, but you better stop eye-fucking my wife like that," Zaire threatened playfully. Joey threw his hands in the air like he was surrendering.

"My bad, bro. I don't want no problems, you know I'll never disrespect you like that, but your wife is beautiful."

"Nigga, I know that. Why the hell you think I married her?" Zaire replied. They all just laughed.

"You look beautiful sis," Brandon, complemented.

"Thanks, bro. You looking good yourself in that all white." Brandon introduced us to his friend that he was with.

"Nyla, this my friend Leah. Leah, these are my sisters, Nyla and Ariel.

"Wait, don't I know you from somewhere," the girl Leah asked Ariel.

"Yeah, cuz, this my girl," Jasmine chimed in. I just giggled because the world was truly small. We all shared small talk before I was sitting down and I was starting to get nauseous again.

"Bestie, you good?" Tasha asked.

"Yeah, I'm good. I wasn't feeling good since earlier today. I thought I was good, but I'm sitting my ass down because I'm trying to get some dick tonight," I told her.

"Bitch, how you sick and talking about getting some dick? I guess I done rubbed off on you. Well, I hope you feel better. Me and Cameron about to go home and get it in while we have a sitter for the night," Tasha said, giving me a hug.

The night was finally over, and I was ready to go home. As soon as me and Zaire made it in the house, we went at it. We never made it pass the living room.

My husband wasn't lying when he said he was gonna fuck the shit out of me when we got in. Zaire was on some other shit tonight. I wasn't even ready for his dick game tonight.

Once we were finished, once again, I had to throw up. I ran to the bathroom, and Zaire came in and stood there with a smirk on his face. I wasn't sure what the fuck was so funny about me puking up my insides. When I got up, I washed my mouth out, and now I had to use the bathroom.

"Here take this," Zaire said, handing me what looked like a pregnancy test. I looked at Zaire like his ass was crazy.

"Why are you giving me this?" I asked.

"Because your ass is pregnant, Nyla. That's why," he answered seriously.

"Nigga, are you crazy? I am not pregnant."

"Well, prove it," he said with a sly smirk that I wanted to smack off his face.

I snatched the test out of his hand, and I couldn't wait to prove him wrong because I knew I wasn't pregnant. I peed on the stick and sat it on the sink and washed my hands as I waited for the negative results. I picked up the test and damn near had a heart attack when I read the word pregnant.

"This can't be right," I mumbled.

"What it say?" Zaire asked, being smart. I just rolled my eyes at his sarcastic ass. He let out a chuckle.

'I can't believe this shit, I need another test," I told him.

"I knew you would say that, so I brought a few of them, but it don't matter how many you take. They all gonna be positive," he said so sure of himself. "Take it in the morning when you wake up. Morning piss is more accurate."

I just shook my head and got in the bed and thought about how my life was about to change if I was really pregnant.

Epilogue

One year later

Candace

I've been battling this cancer for quite some time, and the doctor told me last week that they were only giving me six more months to live. I decided not to tell my boys because they were so happy, and the last thing I needed was for them to neglect their families to count the days that would that I would be dying. I loved them too much for that. The only two people that knew my time was almost up was Charles and my sister Pat. My husband couldn't come to terms with it. Me, on the other hand, wasn't ready to die, but I had come to peace with it.

I know I fought a good fight, so that's all I could do. I mean, I could have longer or I could have a shorter time to live because God has the last say so. I just made sure that every day that I woke up, I lived my best life. I made sure to make it count for something. The truth was I was leaving it in God's hands. I was just happy to see my sons so happy. They had good women that I was sure would hold them down and help them get through my death, so I knew they would be in good hands.

Ariel

"Come on, baby. We gonna be late for our flight," Jasmine yelled up the steps.

"I'm coming, I'm just making sure that I have everything," I yelled back down.

Jasmine and I were still rocking with one another. We were gonna be rocking for a lifetime since we got married last month. We decided to move to Atlanta and start fresh. We decided not to have any kids of our own, but we planned to be dope ass Godparents. We just wanted to enjoy one another and travel. I was scared to be away from my family at first because we've never been separated, but I had to live for me. Besides, we would only be a plane ticket away. Surprisingly, Nyla and Brandon were both happy for me, but of course, Nyla sensitive ass took it hard and cried for damn near two days when I told them I was leaving. I was dragging my feet because my ass was tired. Brandon and Nyla threw me the biggest damn going away party anyone could ask for at Zaire's lounge.

I finally made it downstairs, grabbed my purse and cell phone and headed out the door to the airport. On the way to the airport, I sent everyone a text letting them know I would text them when I land. I also sent them my flight details. When we got to the airport, all I could do was cry when I saw everyone already at the airport to see me off. It was moments like this that made it hard to leave.

After giving my brother and sister the longest hugs in the world, it was time to board the plane. I was officially about to start my new journey with me and my wife.

Brandon

I was sitting at the doctor's office with Leah, waiting to find out if we were having a boy or girl. That's right, your boy is about to be a father, and I know that the baby is mine this time for sure. Leah was my ride or die, and even though she and I have only been together for almost a year, I knew Leah for a few years now. We chilled here and there but never crossed that line. Besides Leah being Jasmine's cousin, she was also Joey's girl best friend. Shit with me and Leah was moving kinda quick, but I knew she was the one for me, so I married her. I didn't want nothing big, so I got married in my backyard then had a bomb ass reception. When the doctor called us back, we got right to business and I was glad because I was excited. The doctor put the ultrasound machine on Leah's belly, and I could see my baby on the screen.

"Congratulations, it's a boy."

I yelled in excitement loudly and scared the damn doctor. That was all I needed. I had my wife, and now I was about to have a son. I couldn't wait to tell Nyla and Ariel. I wish I could tell them together in person, but that ain't gonna happen with Ariel being in Atlanta. I guess I better download Zoom so we can all video chat. After we left the doctors, me and Leah decided to go out to my parents' grave and tell them first then we were gonna stop by her parents' house and tell them.

Cameron

I couldn't believe that mom died. That shit was hard when it first happened, and I felt like somebody took a part of my life. My mom wrote everyone a letter before she died, but she instructed Charles not to give it to us until she's been buried for at least a month. I'm still hurting, and I miss her every day. But her letter did help me deal with her death better. Plus, I had Tasha and my baby girl to get through it. I stopped working as an accountant because it turned out that I was rich. That nigga Brad, wasn't much of a father while he was alive, but he was a pretty good father now that he was dead. Apparently, he had a thirty-million-dollar life insurance policy, and it was instructed that a year after his death myself, Zaire and Brian was to get five million apiece, and my aunt was to get fifteen million. So, I was great in the money department. Plus, I had my own money on top of it. My daughter or any other kids

I have will never want for a damn thing. Now that my mom was gone, I was ready to move. I just didn't know where I wanted to move to, but I knew I was leaving Jersey.

Tasha

So much has happened over the last year that I don't even know where to start. I guess I'll start with I decided to forgive my mom. Thanks to mom Candace and that was the best thing I could have done. My mom was actually cool as shit, and I see where I get my mouth from. Serenity just loved her, and she loved Serenity with everything in her. I still get upset that she wasn't always around, but I learned to appreciate her now. I also built a little relationship with my dad. It was hard to avoid him when he was married to my mother in law. Me and Cameron was over there all the time in her last days. Watching her losing her life made me realize that life was too short for grudges. So, I took the initiative to get to know him, and I hate to admit it, but he was pretty cool too. Cameron and I was going stronger than ever. We were going so strong that he made an honest woman out of me and made me Mrs. Price.

I've been married for six months, and I still couldn't believe that I was somebody's wife. I think the conversations with Mom Candace was what pushed him to marry me. Serenity kept me on my toes chasing her around all day. She was already a mess and she was only almost two. But I can see that me and Cameron's genes together created a hot mess. I made sure to be there for Cameron every minute that he needed me when Ms. Candace passed away. That day broke my heart. I couldn't imagine what he was going through to be honest because I missed her every day, and she wasn't even my biological mom. But he was dealing with it better with every day that passed. So that's it for me. I'm just living my best married life.

Zaire

Losing my mom evoked so many different emotions in me. And I was really grateful for my wife. Nyla was everything that a man could ask for. I was happy that I was the man that got to marry her. Nyla's been my rock and that's just what I needed. My wife deserved the world and I was going to give it to her. If it wasn't for her, I don't know how much more fucked up I would be over my mom. Don't get me wrong, me and Cameron was there for one another, but our wives helped us to get through. I miss my mom every day, but I knew I would be okay as long as I had Nyla. My lounge was doing so great that I opened a few of them. I also had my own clothing line, and I still wrote songs that was hitting the top of the charts. I guess it's safe to say that besides losing my mom, I was living my best life. I was a rich family man with a terrific wife. What else could I ask for?

Nyla

"Zaire, come get your twins," I yelled upstairs.

That's right, you heard me. I had a set of twin girls, Harmony and Symphony. The night I pissed on the stick and found out I was pregnant; the crazy thing was I was already three months pregnant. I had no clue because I was still getting my period every month. My girls were the best thing that ever happened to me. It wasn't easy having twins, but I had plenty of help. Plus, Zaire was a terrific father. He had those girls so spoiled that it didn't make no sense. My mother in law was happy. She was alive to see her grandbabies enter the world. Her death broke everyone's heart. My husband was doing the best he could to deal with it, but it was a struggle. But I had his back no matter what and he had mine.

I was sad to see my sister move, but she was doing great. Ariel's birthday was next week, and we all planned to fly out there and surprise her. I couldn't wait because I missed my sister so much. And as y'all already heard, Tasha was now my sister in law, so life was great on my end. It could only get better from here. I now had four different safe haven centers for rape victims, and they were running great. I loved doing what I did. I was glad women had a safe place to go to get help and counseling with no cost to them whatsoever. So, I guessed everything worked out for the best. God will allow something to happen to you, so He could later use you and your story to help someone else. In my case, I was helping hundreds of women, and I was glad I could. Just like God put me and Zaire together to tell a powerful love story someday. If he didn't, why else would I have accidentally married my rapist? And even once I found out, we were in love, and I decided to stay married to the man that stole my innocence. And I don't regret it not one bit.

The End...

Are you in search of a good publishing home?
Tyanna Presents just may be the perfect place for you!

We are currently accepting submissions in the following genres:

URBAN FICTION
URBAN ROMANCE
WOMEN'S FICTION
STREET LIT
BWWM
PARANORMAL
EROTICA
SUSPENSE

For consideration, please submit the first 3 chapters of your manuscript to:

TYANNAPRESENTS1@GMAIL.COM

To keep up with Author Tyanna
and Tyanna Presents...

Release dates

Live book discussions

Sneak Peeks

Games

Talks with the Author

Cover reveals

Prizes

Please join my reading group...
@Facebook: Tyanna Literary Divas

CPSIA information can be obtained
at www.ICGtesting.com
Printed in the USA
LVHW091608061120
670968LV00002B/271

9 798653 981388